BORDER GOLD

Texas Ranger Gil Palmer has orders to bring in bandit El Lobo — The Wolf, leader of a band of Mexican outlaw raiders — dead or alive. In the town of El Grande, he joins up with Alison and Keith Knox, travelling west on the trail of their grandfather's Spanish gold. As their journey unfolds, Gil discovers that he has a rival suitor for the red-headed Alison. And before the end of the trail, he will face the wrath of El Lobo in a bloody fight to the death . . .

SYDNEY J. BOUNDS

◆

BORDER GOLD

Complete and Unabridged

LINFORD
Leicester

First published in Great Britain in 1952
as *Border Gold* by James Marshal

First Linford Edition
published 2016

A catalogue record for this book is available
from the British Library.

ISBN 978–1–4448–2714–9

Published by
F. A. Thorpe (Publishing)
Anstey, Leicestershire

Set by Words & Graphics Ltd.
Anstey, Leicestershire
Printed and bound in Great Britain by
T. J. International Ltd., Padstow, Cornwall

This book is printed on acid-free paper

1

The lone rider following the stream south appeared in no hurry. He sat his horse, a big roan, with the ease of a man born to the saddle, but his eyes were restless, forever searching the trail for sign, spearing the wooded sides of the watershed for enemies. Behind him, and to the east, stretched the cattle plains of Texas; to the west, the Sacramento Mountains reared against a hot blue sky; before him, the tiny stream wound through arroyos on its way to join the Rio Grande.

He was tall in the saddle, a big-boned man with plenty of muscle and hard sinew, dressed in a grey flannel shirt with a faded blue neckerchief. His leather chaps were worn and a coating of dust covered the polish of his riding boots; the twin Colt .45s belted at his waist had the air of long service.

Shadowed by the wide brim of a stetson hat, Gil Palmer's face was tanned the colour of dark walnut; an interesting face, but not handsome. He was lantern-jawed, with thick lips and protruding cheekbones; his hair was dark and curly, tinged with grey at the sides, and his eyes were clear blue.

Gil travelled light. There was a Winchester jogging his right knee, a water canteen on the other side; his saddle roll contained two blankets, Indian corn and ammunition for his guns. In his shirt pocket was a tobacco pouch and his badge of office, a silver star in a silver circle — a Texas Ranger doesn't advertise the fact when he rides a lone trail after such a dangerous bandit as El Lobo, The Wolf.

Another tributary joined the stream south to the Rio Grande. The roan splashed through it, hoofs clattering on pebbles on the bed of the stream. His eyes were keen, his movements wary; he was close to the border, El Lobo's territory, and his life would not be worth a spent cartridge if he were caught.

Gil remembered what his chief had said: 'Palmer, I'm sending you south. El Lobo's riding again, terrorising the border — I've a pile of letters on my desk, from all along the Rio Grande, asking for help. I know this job calls for a posse, but I can't spare any more men, the way things are at present. So you'll ride a lone trail, and bring in El Lobo — dead or alive!'

Gil hadn't said anything. He'd wondered what his chances of coming back would be — and decided they weren't worth betting his shirt on. The border country was tough and the law new; along the Rio Grande, all disputes were settled at gun-point and a lynching rarely had the sheriff's authority behind it.

'I can't tell you much about El Lobo,' the chief had said. 'We know he's a renegade white man, a tough hombre with brains and the daring to carry out his plans. He leads a band of Mexican outlaws, raiding the cattle ranches and robbing the stages. His hideout is either across the border, or in the mountains to the west — no one knows for sure. No man has seen his face and lived to tell about it.

'I suggest you strike for El Grande, Palmer; and watch out for Velasquez, The Wolf's right-hand man — he's a greaser, tall and lean with a hooked nose, and a gash down the left side of his face that's taken half his ear away. You won't mistake Valasquez, and where you find him, El Lobo won't be far away.'

The chief had grinned and shook him by the hand.

'Good luck, Palmer — and don't come back till you can tell me El Lobo's days are over and the Rio Grande is safe for honest men.'

Gil Palmer saddled his roan and started south for El Grande. He took his time and kept his eyes open, watching for sign and the men who would try to kill him. He followed the

4

stream as it flowed south to the Rio Grande, the border between Texas and Mexico, El Lobo's country.

Beyond the next line of bluff, he came upon his first view of El Grande. The border town nestled in a natural hollow between the hills, with wooden shacks sprawling out from a zig-zag Main Street; there were few brick and adobe buildings, and only Main Street had a boardwalk. Gil rode unhurriedly into town, noting the high proportion of Mexicans, the two saloons and single hotel. He hitched the roan beside horses with a Bar 77 brand and stared up Main Street, unconsciously hitching his guns as hostile eyes settled on him.

Gil booked a room at the hotel and ate at the dining-rooms opposite. His hunger satisfied, he rolled and lit a cigarette and lounged on the board-walk. He wanted news of El Lobo and the place where tongues were loosest was the saloons; he looked first at Murdoch's Bar, a wooden building faced with gilt paint and scarred with bullet holes, then passed on to Smoky Joe's.

The second saloon was smaller, dingier than Murdoch's Bar, but despite this, the crowd was larger. An out-of-tune piano sounded between the clink of glasses and the murmur of voices; Smoky Joe's seemed the more popular of the two saloons with the inhabitants of El Grande, and that fact intrigued Gil.

He pushed through the batwing doors, into Smoky Joe's. The floor was covered with sawdust that hadn't been renewed for a week and the light filtering through dirty windows was dim — but it was still bright enough for Gil to see he'd walked into a stick-up.

★　★　★

Two riders headed south for El Grande by the old cattle trail. The girl took the lead, head held high. She was in her early twenties, pretty, with red hair and a determined tilt to her chin; her eyes too, a magnificent tawny, showed that she had plenty of spirit. Her riding dress, obviously new and tricked out with beads and fancy leather-work, proclaimed her as recently arrived from the east.

Alison Knox turned her head and looked into her brother's pale and scowling face. He was three years younger and soft with easy living; his chin lacked firmness and his eyes were dull — he seemed to have none of his sister's fire and determination. For a moment, she frowned, then her gaze softened.

'Not much further, Keith,' she said encouragingly, 'then you'll be able to rest. El Grande can't be more than three or four miles now.'

Keith Knox scowled at his sister. He rode awkwardly in the saddle of his Indian pony and felt tired and hot and dusty. It had seemed fun, at first, to dress up like a cowboy and set out for the West, but days of hardship on the prairie had frayed his nerves.

'It was a crazy idea to leave Richmond,' he burst out. 'I'm sick of riding this stupid horse and living rough. Old Seth Knox must have been out of his mind when he came out here to look for a lost treasure. I'll bet it never existed and the old man's dead — Alison, let's turn back after we've rested at El Grande.'

The girl frowned again. She knew the extent of her brother's weakness, what little protection he would be if danger threatened on the trail.

'You were keen enough to set out,' she said. 'The thought of laying your hands on some easy money suited you — I don't suppose you spared a thought for grandfather. Why, he might be lying desperately ill in some remote part — '

'We'd have heard,' Keith Knox said shortly. 'He'd have got a message back somehow.'

Alison made no reply. She thought of her grandfather as she rode the grey pony towards El Grande. It was five years since he had set out on the trail of a fabulous treasure and, during all that time, they had received no news of him. An old map he had discovered showed the location of a gold cache carried north by the Indians, three centuries back, as they fled before the Spanish invaders; Seth Knox, with three associates, had set out to find the treasure — and had not returned.

Keith thought only of finding the gold; Alison of learning what had happened to her grandfather. So they had travelled west as far as the railroad went, then bought horses and started the long ride to El Grande. It was there that Seth Knox had set out on the treasure trail; there he had said he would leave word of his progress, in case he should not return.

El Grande showed as a huddle of shacks in the distance and Keith used his quirt on the pony. It broke into a canter and he passed Alison shouting:

'At last, a place where we can get beds and a decent meal. I'm going to sleep for a week before going back east.'

Alison smiled thinly; she had no intention of turning back before she learnt what had happened to her grandfather — and she didn't think Keith would make the return journey alone. He would grumble, but even he couldn't leave her alone, unprotected, in this wild country where the only law was gun-law.

Amused faces watched them ride down Main Street. To the hardened men of the West, these two greenhorns were heading for trouble. One or two men laughed at their garb; Alison got admiring glances, for a pretty girl was a rarity in the border country. Keith noticed the way men's eyes stopped on his sister, and he straightened up in the saddle, his hand dropping to the gun at his waist. His manner developed a swagger as he realised he might have to protect Alison from unwanted attentions.

Keith's patronising manner alarmed Alison; she knew her brother would not stand a chance in a gunfight with these men of the West, and she hoped she could avert trouble for him on her account. Nevertheless, it gave her a warm feeling for him that he should show he wanted to protect her. She forgave him for showing weakness on the trail.

Alison watched the names on the shop-fronts till she saw the place she wanted: Smoky Joe's saloon. Seth Knox had corresponded with Smoky Joe before setting out for El Grande; it was here he had said he would leave his last message. Alison dismounted and hitched her pony to the wooden rail outside the saloon; Keith followed her in through swing doors, up to the bar.

A piano sounded a little out of tune and glasses clinked. Four punchers were playing poker at a table; their eyes raised and followed Alison as she went to the bar. She saw the bartender, a short, bald man with a dirty apron round his middle; his face looked like that of an honest man.

He beamed at her, and said: 'Smoky Joe at your service, ma'am. What's your pleasure?'

He wiped his hands on a cloth, his eyes passing from the girl to the tenderfoot at her side. He frowned at the way the youngster's hand closed round the butt of a Colt; Smoky Joe didn't like the idea of gun-play in his saloon and, if he read the signs right, this kid was asking for trouble.

'I'm Alison Knox, and this is my brother Keith,' the girl said. 'Our grandfather, Seth Knox, was here about five years ago. You'll remember him — he left a message for us.'

Smoky Joe looked at them more closely.

'You can prove who you are?' he challenged.

Alison showed a locket suspended from her neck; she opened it to reveal three miniatures, one each of Keith and herself, the third that of a weather-beaten man in his late fifties, with a straggling moustache and keen eyes. His chin had the same forceful thrust as Alison's.

Smoky Joe smiled and nodded.

'I reckon you're who you say you are,' he drawled. 'Old Seth left a letter — I'll get it — but' — he squinted at Alison — 'if you had hopes of seeing your grandpa again, forget them. If he was still alive, he'd have showed up before this. The border country is wild and a man's life ain't worth a damn out here. I guess he's sure passed on to his Maker.'

He disappeared into a back room behind the bar counter, returning with a sealed envelope, dingy-grey with dirty thumb marks.

'I guess this here is yourn,' he grunted. 'Seth wrote it the night before he left El Grande. He said I was to hold it in trust for his descendants, if they ever showed up — and he never came back.'

Alison recognised her grandfather's handwriting on the envelope, and

13

suddenly wanted to cry. Keith remembered the gold that Seth Knox had been after — maybe there was something to the story. He pushed forward and grabbed the letter.

A voice said: 'I'll take that.' Keith turned to see the two men who had come in. They were both tough-looking hombres and the set-up smelled of trouble.

★ ★ ★

Jamie Riggs had been trailing Alison and Keith Knox for days. He kept well back, out of sight, cursing them for their slowness; Jamie was a hardrider, a man with a price on his head, and he was used to travelling far and fast. It irked him to be forced to slow his pace to that of a couple of greenhorns, but he wanted to be sure of their determination.

When it became obvious they were heading for El Grande, he spurred his horse to a fast canter and struck off the old cattle trail. He made a wide circle to pass the two riders without being seen, picked up the trail ahead of them, and rode into El Grande.

Jamie dismounted outside Murdoch's saloon, hitched his gelding to the rack and looked around him. Though he had never been in El Grande before, he was familiar with the layout of small western towns; they were all much the same. Jamie scowled in the direction of the sheriff's office, then turned his attention to the front of Murdoch's Bar.

To his practised eye, it was evident that Murdoch was a man of importance in El Grande. Jamie smiled thinly; he thought Murdoch would be the man he wanted. He clumped up the steps to the boardwalk and pushed through the batwing doors.

The wooden walls were gilt-painted, the floor covered with clean sawdust except for a raised platform at the back; Jamie guessed it served as a stage for dancing girls. In one corner, three punchers sat throwing dice; at another table a poker school played in the tense silence that indicated high stakes. The bar ran the length of one wall, a long cedarwood counter with a polished brass footrail.

His eyes moved back to the poker school and he studied the four men sitting there, wrapped in silence. One man alone impressed him; a granite-faced man dressed in black. His hair was long but trimmed, and he sported sideboards. A long cheroot jutted from his mouth and night-black eyes stared fixedly before him. Despite the paleness of his skin, this man held an aura of power; Jamie guessed this was the man he sought.

He moved forward and stood behind the man in black, looking down at the cards he held, at the pile of coin and notes in the centre of the table.

Jamie said: 'If you're Murdoch, I want a pow-wow with yuh in private.'

The man in black raised his eyes and stared coldly at Jamie; two gunmen

16

moved in behind Jamie, the gambler's bodyguard.

'I'm Murdoch — and I'm busy. There's big money on this hand.'

Jamie looked at the money, rapidly estimated the amount in the pot, and jeered:

'Five hundred bucks! And I thought I was talking to the big man in this town. I've got a proposition for yuh, one with real money attached — ' He lowered his voice so that only Murdoch should hear: 'Maybe as much as a hundred thousand bucks!'

Murdoch shifted in his seat, placing his cards face-down on the table. As he moved, his coat swung open, showing the long-barrelled Colt holstered under his armpit. His black eyes bored into Jamie's face, read there the hunted look of a wanted man.

'I guess the sheriff will be interested in you, stranger.'

Jamie smiled; he knew he had Murdoch's interest. He hadn't mistaken his man.

'Do we have that private talk?' he said softly. 'Do I look like a man who'll run around wet behind the ears?'

Murdoch looked at Jamie, noting the low-slung .45s, the marks of the professional gunman, the weather-lined face and gnarled hands. Jamie was on the short side, with untidy hair and a cleft chin; his stained shirt and ragged chaps told he was a hombre who spent more time travelling for his health than most, but Murdoch felt he was a man who knew what he was talking about.

The gambler stood up, pushed in his cards. 'I'm throwing in my hand,' he said, turning his back on the table. He motioned to Jamie: 'This way.'

They went back of the saloon and up a flight of wooden stairs, to a room overlooking Main Street. Jamie went across to the window and looked out, watching the trail into town. There was no sign of the two greenhorns yet.

Murdoch said: 'You got a name?'

'Jamie Riggs — your sheriff will likely

have a handbill describing me, if you're interested.'

Murdoch flicked ash from his cheroot, smiling thinly.

'I run El Grande — and the sheriff. You got no cause to worry about the law here, Riggs.'

Jamie nodded. 'I figgered it that way. You're the big shot around here, and I reckoned I'd run up against yuh some time, so I came in to make a deal. Back my play, and we'll split fifty-fifty.'

He paused, watching Murdoch closely.

'Keep talking. You mentioned a hundred thousand. That's a helluva lot o' money for these parts.'

Jamie watched the street again, rolled a quirly and lit up.

'I came across some papers left by a man named Harper; he was hunting a lost treasure with three other hombres, Seth Knox, Cassidy, and Flint.

'It seems that Knox got hold of a map showing the location of a gold cache, brought north by the Indians way back when Indians were history. They started out from El Grande — and haven't been heard of since. That means they're dead — I'm sure Harper is — and we've got a clear trail. Knox was leaving clues to follow; all we got to do is step in and take the treasure.'

Murdoch frowned, stubbing out his cheroot.

'I've heard stories like this before, gold caches and silver mines, though the Indian angle is a new one on me. I heard a rumour about Knox, but he was before my time. What makes you so sure there's something in it?'

Jamie pointed through the window. Murdoch saw two riders coming into town from the north.

'Alison and Keith Knox,' Jamie said. 'They ain't come all this way for their health. I reckon they've got a lead — and I aim to cut in on them.'

Murdoch stared down the street as the riders passed by. His eyes fixed on Alison and he smiled unpleasantly.

'Maybe this treasure doesn't exist,' he said, 'but that girl sure does. And I aim to make her acquaintance. Let's go, Riggs.'

Jamie followed him down the stairs. Murdoch shook his head at the bodyguard and stepped on to the boardwalk, outside the saloon. He saw Alison and Keith tie up their ponies and enter Smoky Joe's; he frowned — Smoky Joe was a thorn in Murdoch's side. He ran an honest bar and attracted a lot of business; Murdoch had been unable to shift him out of El Grande. If Knox had left a message, it would likely be at Smoky Joe's.

'Keep with me, Riggs,' he ordered. 'And no gunplay — unless I say so. Then shoot fast and shoot to kill.'

He reached the batwings of Smoky Joe's and went inside. Alison was showing a locket to the bartender. Murdoch grabbed Jamie's arm and signalled him to be still; they waited. Smoky Joe went back of the counter and returned with a letter. Keith Knox leant forward to grab it.

Murdoch moved quickly. 'I'll take that!'

Keith swung round, reaching for his gun. Murdoch laughed.

'Take him, Riggs!'

Jamie spread his legs; his mouth tightened in a bitter line and his close-set eyes narrowed for the kill. Almost he laughed; this kid was going to be easy. He went for his guns —

Alison flung herself in front of her brother, covering him with her slim young form. Jamie hesitated as Murdoch's voice barked.

'Not the girl! Don't kill the girl!'

Alison held her head high, red hair flowing behind her, chin stuck out, tawny eyes flashing; she wondered if this was her last moment.

★ ★ ★

No one saw Gil Palmer push through the swing doors into Smoky Joe's saloon; all eyes were on the tableau at

22

the bar. The piano stopped abruptly and the poker players scattered as Jamie Riggs went for his guns. Gil tensed; he'd seen men of this type before, professional killers, who hired out their guns for ready money. The man in black with sideboards and piercing eyes had the mark of a gambler, coldly calculating and unyielding in his desires; the girl and the kid were obviously greenhorns, caught in a deadly trap.

Gil saw the girl throw herself in front of the youngster, heard the man in black call:

'Not the girl! Don't kill the girl!'

Gil's eyes filled with admiration for her courage; she shielded the kid with head held high. Then his hands swept through short arcs to his gun-butts; twin Colts jumped into his hands and his fingers were taut on the triggers. His voice was harsh:

'I got the drop on yuh hombres — '

Jamie spun round; his eyes met Gil's — and wavered. He let his guns drop back in their holsters and his hands fall free at his side. He swore at Gil and looked to Murdoch for help. Murdoch smiled thinly; he had the letter in his hand that he'd grabbed from Keith Knox — all he wanted now was to get clear with it. He swaggered forward, eyeing Gil boldly.

'Stranger,' he said, 'you're interfering in something that ain't your business, and that's unhealthy in these parts. For your information, I'm Neil Murdoch and I own most of El Grande. I'd advise that you hit the trail, pronto.'

'Right this minute,' Gil clipped, 'I'm holding the ace in the stack. Give that letter back to the girl.'

Murdoch hesitated. He stared into Gil's blue eyes, and what he saw there made him uneasy. Murdoch shrugged and held out the letter. Alison took it without a word.

'Now beat it,' Gil snapped. 'And don't show your face in here again tonight, unless you want me gunning for yuh!'

Jamie started for the door. Murdoch followed him, paused at the batwings.

'We'll meet again, stranger — and next time I'll be calling the play.'

He followed Jamie out into the street and the swing door closed behind them. Gil waited, guns in hand, in case they should try a shot through the window; but nothing happened. Gil holstered his guns, removed his stetson and bowed to Alison.

'Gil Palmer's the name, ma'am, and I'm glad to have been of service.'

She smiled and took a step forward, holding out her hand.

'I'm Alison Knox, and this is my brother Keith. We're obliged to you, Mister Palmer.'

Gil thought she was the prettiest girl he'd seen in a long time. Something of this must have shown in his eyes, for she lowered her gaze as he took her hand. She admired the set of his shoulders, the clear blue of his eyes, and the tan of his skin; she felt she was in the presence of a real man.

Keith's face was white, and he felt the need to assert himself. He blustered:

'There was no call for you to interfere, Palmer. I'm quite capable of looking after my sister.'

Gil looked at him. He wondered how a girl with so much courage could have a brother as soft and weak as this. His voice was level as he replied:

'In the West, youngster, we don't reckon to let a woman shield us from danger. I'd advise yuh to learn to use that iron you're carrying — or leave it off!'

Keith flushed. Smoky Joe pushed a drink towards Gil.

'On the house,' the bartender drawled. 'It ain't every day an hombre gets the drop on Murdoch and makes him crawl. It did my eyes good to watch.'

Gil took the glass and drained it; the warming effect of the whisky took some of the tension out of him, and he realised he'd been near to killing a man.

Though he'd killed rustlers and murderers in the line of duty, Gil had never been able to achieve the cold-blooded indifference that marks a professional gunslinger. He always tried to carry out his orders without a gunfight, and, when he had to shoot or be shot, it was in a kind of nervous sweat; he fought not only his opponent, but his conscience, too. Though he was born to the ways of the West, and knew it must always be the man with the gun who carried the law into bandit territory, he felt it was a terrible thing to take another man's life. That he had been prepared to do so on Alison Knox's account, unsettled him. No other girl he had met exerted such power over him.

He put down the empty glass and looked thoughtfully at Smoky Joe.

'Murdoch's the big man around here, I guess?'

The bartender shrugged. 'He owns most of El Grande, but he ain't popular. Most punchers around here use this bar instead of Murdoch's. He's got too many hired killers around him and no one ever brought their winnings out of his saloon. Some say he's behind a lot of the crimes that go on in these parts, but whatever the truth about that, he's a dangerous man to cross. If you're staying long in El Grande, Palmer, I'd advise yuh to watch your step.'

Gil turned to Alison.

'You staying on in El Grande?' he asked. 'I reckon you'll be needing a little help, seeing as you've already run up against Murdoch.'

Keith snarled: 'Mind your own business!'

Alison turned on her brother. 'Really, Keith — Mr Palmer saved your life just now. That's no way to speak to him.' She addressed Gil: 'I should be glad of any help you can give us. You see, we're looking for — '

Smoky Joe held up his hand.

'I've a private room at the back you can use,' he said. 'No sense in talking here, where everyone can listen in. I reckon too many know already,' he added, thinking of Jamie Riggs.

The bartender left a man in charge of the saloon and led Alison and Gil to a small room. Keith Knox followed, obviously annoyed with his sister for bringing a stranger into their affairs.

Alison said: 'I'd like you to stay, Joe. You can tell us something about my grandfather's stay here.'

She opened the letter, and read aloud:

'My dear grandchildren,
'If you receive this letter, which I write before setting out on the treasure trail, you must accept that I am no longer of this world. The country I am going into, with Flint, Harper and Cassidy, is wild and dangerous; nevertheless the lure of fabulous riches draws us on. Briefly, the story is this:
'Back in 1519, when Hernando Cortès invaded Mexico and seized

Montezuma II, the Aztec ruler, a band of Indians collected all the sacred treasures on which they could lay their hands, and fled north before the Spanish invaders. These treasures, which were wrought in silver and gold, the Aztecs carried into the land which is now Texas, and there hid. The Spaniards died of exposure and disease, and for three centuries, the treasure has been lost from human eye.

'I came into possession of a map, which I believe to be a true guide to the location of the sacred treasures of the Aztecs, and with my associates, intend to search until we find them. If we are successful, we shall be rich beyond the dreams of men — if we fail, you're not likely to see me again on this earth.

'In the event of failure, I leave this letter with Smoky Joe (an honest man), so that you may

30

know the full truth. I shall leave a trail which you can follow, if you so wish, and the thought of danger and death does not deter you from my footsteps. If you succeed where I fail, I shall know that you are true descendants of the pioneers who blazed the western trails of our glorious country. Tomorrow we set out for Sagebush, where I shall leave the next clue for you to follow. My last wish is for your happiness.

'Your loving grandfather,

'SETH KNOX.'

As Alison finished reading and laid down the letter, there was a long moment of silence, then Smoky Joe drawled:

'If you'll take my advice, Miss Knox, you'll forget about the treasure and go back east. Old Seth wasn't underestimating the dangers on the trail — and it's obvious he and his partners were killed, either by outlaws or the wild country they had to cross.'

Keith's face was white. His voice had a bitter ring to it.

'We're going back!'

Alison blazed up: 'I'm not. I'll go on alone if necessary — grandfather gave his life to find this treasure and I'm going to carry on where he left off. Keith can go back if he likes — but I'm riding for Sagebush, and the next clue, in the morning.'

Keith scowled. 'You know I won't leave you to go on alone, sis. If you're set on the trip to Sagebush, I'll come with you. But I think it's crazy.'

Gil spoke his thoughts aloud.

'I'm admiring yuh for wanting to go through with the business, Miss Knox, but I'm figgering yuh would be wise to call it off. This here is a rough country' — he waved his hands vaguely towards distant vistas — 'desert and mountain, populated by wild animals and bad men. Too, there's Murdoch and his outfit to consider; they're after yuh, all right. And Jamie Riggs; he's a bad one and obviously knows about the treasure — why else should they show so much interest in your grandfather's letter? You set eyes on this Riggs before, Joe?'

'Never. But there ain't no doubt he's a wrong 'un.'

Gil studied the glowing tip of his cigarette, speaking softly. 'Then there's El Lobo to consider. I hear The Wolf's riding again — you hear about that, Joe?'

'El Lobo?' Alison repeated in surprise.

'Not so loud,' Smoky Joe cautioned. 'There's plenty of greasers in El Grande and it would surprise me mighty if a few of them aren't in The Wolf's pay.' He explained for Alison's benefit: 'El Lobo is a renegade white man, an outlaw with a price on his head, and he leads a band of Mexican bandits, plundering the border country for miles around. There ain't nothing bad enough for that hombre to stop at — and it would be mighty unpleasant for you if he got onto this treasure trail.

Even Murdoch don't rove far from El Grande, on account o' The Wolf.'

Keith Knox sneered: 'A renegade white man? That couldn't be you, Palmer?'

Gil smiled; that would amuse the chief — if he ever got back to tell him. Smoky Joe said:

'If Palmer was El Lobo, son, you'd be a candidate for Boot Hill right this minute. I'm advising yuh to fit a bridle over that run-away tongue o' yourn.'

'Yes, shut up, Keith,' Alison said. 'Please excuse my brother, Mr Palmer. The trip here has upset him — he's not used to roughing it.'

Gil grinned. 'I can see that!'

'If you're free, Mr Palmer, I'd like you to join us. I feel you'd be a considerable asset in the dangers ahead. Of course, you'll get a share of the treasure if we find it. And if we don't — '

Keith interrupted, scowling at Gil.

'You're crazy, sis. Palmer is just another gunman. If we ever found this treasure, he'd shoot us down in cold blood and take it for himself.'

Gil forced himself to remember it was Alison's brother who spoke.

Alison repeated: 'Will you join us, Mr Palmer?'

Gil considered it. His job was to hunt down El Lobo, not provide an escort for a couple of greenhorns, but he admired the girl's courage and knew that, on their own, they wouldn't last three days once they set out from El Grande. He looked at Alison and thought again how pretty she was. Dressed in her smart eastern riding suit, she made a tremendous appeal to him. He felt he wanted to protect her, he made himself stop thinking of her like that. There was El Lobo to consider —

For a moment, he considered revealing that he was a Texas Ranger, then decided against it. He didn't want El Lobo forewarned, and Keith's tongue was too loose. But Alison would be riding into The Wolf's territory, he argued; he'd be sure to run across the outlaw's trail if he rode with Alison and her brother.

'All right, Miss Knox,' he said slowly. 'I'll join your party. And I'd like it if you'd call me Gil.'

She held out her hand, and said:

'Thank you, Gil. I feel a lot better, knowing you'll be riding with us.'

Keith didn't say anything. Smoky Joe smiled, and looked from Gil to Alison.

'I reckon you'll be all right, miss. I ain't never seen Gil Palmer before, but he showed Murdoch the way out — and that tells me all I want to know about a man. Good luck to yuh.'

Gil walked back to the hotel with Alison and her brother. He said goodnight and walked up to his room.

2

Neil Murdoch sat by the window in his room above the saloon, looking down into Main Street. He was smiling as he watched three riders move away from the stables and head out of El Grande. Jamie Riggs scowled and touched his gun-butts with itching fingertips.

'Yuh going to let them get clear away?' he growled.

Murdoch's eyes travelled back from the slim figure of Alison Knox and fixed on Jamie's face; his night-black eyes regarded the gunman with contempt.

'You don't know me very well yet, Riggs, or you wouldn't ask such a question. But I do these things my way — and in my time. There's no hurry to settle with Palmer — it'll be easier on the trail.'

Jamie was restless; he saw a fortune in treasure slipping through their fingers while Murdoch sat smoking a cheroot and staring after the girl.

'Yuh figgering on trailing them?' he asked. 'That Palmer knows his way around — he ain't going to leave markers all over the place. I reckon we ought to saddle and get after them pronto.'

Murdoch laughed. 'I've had a man watching the hotel all night, Riggs. At dawn, one of my riders went into the hills. Palmer won't be expecting anyone ahead of him; he'll be watching the back trail. Don't worry, we'll know where they go.'

'That's smart,' Jamie acknowledged.

Murdoch drew on his cheroot. 'We're waiting for reinforcements, Riggs. Once we've left El Grande behind, we're in The Wolf's territory. I don't aim to locate this treasure, then fall prey to El Lobo. I'm recruiting sufficient men to take care of those Mexican bandits.'

Jamie turned away from the window as Gil, Alison and Keith passed out of sight. 'You got a head on yuh,' he admitted.

Murdoch chuckled. Jamie was used to riding a lone trail; he hadn't the brain to organise an outfit of his own.

'I didn't get to be boss of El Grande by making fool moves,' Murdoch boasted. 'Gun-law is the only law in the border country and the hombre with most guns behind him is top-man. Palmer's going to find that out before long.'

There was a knock at the door, Murdoch called out for the man to come in. The door opened and a red-faced giant with a stubbled chin entered; he said:

'The boys you want are downstairs, boss. Goin' to talk to them now?'

Murdoch rose from his chair and crushed out the cheroot.

'Yeah, Tex. I'll come down. You, too, Riggs.'

The three men went down to the bar, where a crowd of roughnecks waited. One man, thin and angular with a lean brown face and notched six-guns, detached himself from the mob.

'These boys figger your kind of money hires their guns, boss, but they want to know what it's all about.'

Murdoch said, softly: 'Do they, Slim?'

He looked them over. There were six hombres packing two guns apiece; tough-looking men with the stamp of the outlaw plain in their faces.

Murdoch's tone was harsh as he addressed them.

'Let's get one thing straight; I'm the boss! I pay your wages and you carry out my orders. I've no intention of divulging my plans at present and I'm not answering questions. We're riding into El Lobo's territory and I want you boys along in case we have to argue with the greasers. Any man who objects to following orders blind can stand down now.'

He paused. No one objected. One man grunted:

'As long as we're paid, we don't give

a damn — for El Lobo or anyone else!'

Murdoch relaxed, smiling. 'Riggs, here' — he waved a hand at Jamie — 'is partnering me on this trip. When I'm not around, you'll take your orders from him. That clear?'

The gunmen looked at Jamie and nodded.

Murdoch said: 'One more thing. We're likely to run into a girl, a red-head by the name of Alison Knox — I don't want her harmed.'

Jamie looked at the gambler with disapproval; he didn't like the idea of mixing pleasure with business. Women, to him, were just a source of trouble; still, the set-up looked good. Six gunmen plus Tex and Slim, Murdoch and himself.

Murdoch turned to the bartender: 'Drinks all round — then you boys can check your guns and horses. We'll be riding before long.'

Glasses clinked and liquor splashed freely. Jamie called a toast: 'To a good hunt an — '

Murdoch cut him short with an oath. He'd have to watch Riggs; whisky went to his head and made him talkative — and he didn't want news of this expedition leaking out to El Lobo. Murdoch went back to his room to wait. He lit a cheroot and sat by the window, thinking of Alison's beauty . . . It was past noon when his rider returned, and whispered in his ear, one word:

'Sagebush!'

★　★　★

The sun was high in the sky when El Grande dropped from view behind the line of hills. Alison and Keith Knox rode side by side as their ponies trotted over short grass and through low scrub, windswept and earthy-brown. Gil hung back behind them, watching the trail with sharp eyes; a tiny furrow of puzzlement creased his forehead. He expected to see Murdoch's riders hard on their heels, but the line of the horizon was unbroken except for the dark branches of cedar and cotton-wood.

He caught up with Alison and her brother as they reached a shallow creek.

'Upstream,' Gil said. 'We'll ride as if for the mountains, then double back, walking the horses down the creek to hide our trail. That'll throw Murdoch off the scent for a while.'

Keith was impatient to reach Sage-bush; he didn't enjoy the hard leather saddle of his Indian pony and he wanted to get to the next town and rest.

'I don't see anyone following us,' he said coolly.

Gil let that ride; he joined Alison and headed upstream, picking the way so the horses' tracks kept mainly to rocky soil; he didn't want the trail to be too conspicuous or Murdoch would be suspicious when it petered out. A mile further on, he nosed his roan into the water and turned back. Alison and Keith followed him.

'Keep in the middle of the creek,' Gil

warned. 'That way we shan't disturb the sides of the bank and give the game away.'

They splashed downstream in single file, Gil in the lead. The water was sparkling clear and cool and tiny fish played in pools under the rocks. Gil kept the party to the creek till they were well past the point where they had turned off, then he climbed the bank of the creek and picked up the Sagebush trail again.

From time to time he would stop and shield his eyes from the sun's glare, staring back towards El Grande, but of Murdoch's men he saw no sign. That worried him, for he thought Murdoch wasn't the sort of man to give up without a chase. If he had thought more carefully, he might have guessed that the gambler had sent his spy ahead; but Gil didn't guess — so he missed the hidden watcher.

Now, with Murdoch apparently out of the running, Gil gave his attention to El Lobo. They were moving deeper into

The Wolf's country with every step; alone he would not have worried, but with Alison to protect, he thought it best to reach Sagebush as fast as possible. He gave the order to quicken pace. Keith scowled and grumbled all the while, till his sister lost her temper and told him to shut up. Gil grinned to himself.

They came in sight of Sagebush in the late afternoon. It was smaller than El Grande, but built along similar lines. There didn't seem to be many people about in the hot sun and only a couple of dogs, fighting, rose any dust on Main Street. Gil halted outside the hotel and tethered the roan. Alison and Keith followed him into the shadowy interior.

They had a wash and a meal and rested, talking in low tones.

'What sort of clue would grandfather leave here?' Alison wondered, turning to Gil.

'We'll just have to hunt around. One thing's certain — he wouldn't be leaving another letter. Honest men aren't that easy to find in these parts.'

'I suppose we can ask?' Keith snapped.

'I'd advise against it,' Gil said. 'I reckon the best plan is to split up and wander round the town, using our eyes instead of our tongues. My guess is we'll spot something in a conspicuous place — knowing you'd be along some day. And it would have to be something that wouldn't arouse idle curiosity.'

He rose and jammed on his stetson.

'See you later, Alison.'

He'd suggested splitting up because he had another job to do; he wanted to learn if any of El Lobo's men were in town. But Sagebush was a sleepy place, without a bank, and it appeared that The Wolf rarely bothered the town. Occasionally a few of El Lobo's bandits went on a drinking spree, but there weren't any in town at the moment. For which Gil felt glad — on account of Alison. Though he didn't doubt that The Wolf's spies had sent back a report.

He wandered the few streets, called

in at the only saloon and kept his ears and eyes open. It wasn't till he strolled outside the town that he spotted anything to rouse his interest; he made a circle and arrived back on Main Street as Keith and his sister were going into the hotel.

Alison looked at him with a question in her eyes. Gil nodded and spoke to Keith.

'We'll need a couple of spades. Buy them from the store next to the blacksmith's. If the storeman gets nosey, drop a hint you're going prospecting in the hills.' Gil chuckled. 'He'll write you off as another crazy greenhorn from the east and quit thinking about it.'

For once Keith Knox obeyed without argument; maybe he thought Gil had already discovered the lost treasure and that all they had to do was dig it up.

As darkness fell over Sagebush and long shadows crept over the silent streets, Gil rose and belted on his guns. He picked up the two spades and a shielded oil-lamp he had borrowed from the shed behind the hotel.

'I want you to stay here, Alison,' he said. 'This may be an unpleasant business, and — '

'I'm coming,' the girl said decisively, sticking out her chin.

'What are we going to do?' Keith asked uneasily.

'I took a look at Boot Hill this afternoon. There's a grave there with a wooden cross — and the name carved on the cross is Roger Flint. The name of one of your grandfather's associates. We're going to open the grave — and I expect to find more than a body.'

Keith's face went pale. Alison's lips made a firm line.

'I appreciate your trying to spare my feelings, Gil, but I'm going with you.' She looked at her brother and added: 'I think I'll be more use than Keith.'

Gil hesitated, shrugged when he saw she had made up her mind.

'Maybe you will, at that,' he drawled. 'Anyway, you can stand guard. You don't have to look in the grave — it won't be a pleasant sight after five years.'

He led the way, down dark side streets, to the outskirts of the town. There was no one about; the only noise came from the lighted windows of the saloon on Main Street. Boot Hill stretched from immediately behind some wooden shacks, up a gentle slope, to a cluster of piñon trees. The grass was knee-high and crude wooden crosses jutted from the ground at irregular intervals; further along the grass track earthy mounds marked newer graves.

They walked under the starlight, for the moon had yet to rise, and Gil refused to light the lantern till it was required. Under stunted juniper shrub was the grave Gil had earmarked. The writing on the cross said simply: ROGER FLINT. There was no date.

Gil lit the oil-lamp and set it down in a hollow, screening the light on the side showing towards town. He passed one of the spades to Keith.

Alison said: 'Are you sure we're doing right, Gil?'

'Yep. Old Seth would leave his clue here. It's an old trick, to leave a message in a grave.'

He set to, thrusting the curved blade of the spade into the soil, using his foot to drive it deeper. It had been raining a few days before, and the ground was soft.

Keith started work at the foot of the grave and they worked downward. A foot under the surface the ground became harder, and both men were soon sweating. Keith rested periodically, but Gil continued digging. He was soon up to his knees and lifted the oil-lamp into the shallow pit. Alison waited a little way off, a shadowy figure beneath the trees.

Half an hour later they were four feet down and the smell of decayed flesh told them they were very near the end of their grim business. Keith's face was pale and his eyes glassy; he felt sick and limp. Gil set his lips and ignored the stench, digging deeper, throwing the soil upwards so that it formed a barrier along the edge of the grave.

They came to the body a few minutes later. There was no coffin and the cloth the corpse had been wrapped in had half-rotted away. Keith leant against the wall of earth, moaning. Gil bent down, swinging the lamp the length of the pit and found what he had expected — a small package wrapped in oil-skin.

He tore it open and found a sheet of parchment with the one word: PARADISE.

'It's here, Alison,' Gil called.

She came across and bent over the open grave, averting her eyes from the grisly remains of Roger Flint. Gil handed her the paper and commented:

'Paradise is a small town to the west of here. I guess we'll find the next clue there. We'll — '

He broke off suddenly as a movement in the darkness indicated they had visitors. A harsh voice called:

'This is the end of the trail for you, Palmer. Hand over the paper and I'll let the girl go free. Let him have it, boys!'

Gil grabbed Alison's hand and pulled her down into the pit. 'Murdoch!' he whispered. 'Keep down!'

He drew his Colts and smothered the lamp. Starlight showed shadowy figures lurking in the darkness. Red flame stabbed out and a lead slug buried itself in the pile of earth beside the grave. Gil fired back at the tell-tale flash, ducked as a hail of lead sprayed his way. He bobbed up again, shooting with both guns.

Alison had her brother's gun in her hand; she stood beside Gil, looking for a target. Gil pushed her down again.

'I'll handle this,' he grunted. 'You load the guns.'

Murdoch's voice came again: 'Close in!'

Gil blasted a shot at his voice, but the gambler was keeping under cover, leaving the dangerous work to his hired killers. The darkness was alive with gunshots and searching red flame; Gil kept his guns working till they became hot in his hands; he passed them down, one at a time, and Alison reloaded. Keith crouched in one corner of the grave, white and scared. He muttered:

'Give them the message, Alison — then they'll go away. I'm sick of the whole business. All I want is to get back east with a whole skin.'

'Shut up, Keith! At least you might try to act like a man!'

Gil saw a movement in the starlight and fired at it. An oath told him he'd winged one of their attackers. A barrage of shots forced him to crouch low again; lead shells ricocheted off the mound of earth round the grave. A flying splinter of rock slashed his temple and he felt a trickle of blood run down his cheek, into his mouth.

Murdoch's men were at a disadvantage; they were in the open, afraid to rush the three in the grave because of Gil's deadly marksmanship. Murdoch called again:

'Hand over the clue to the treasure and we'll call the fight off.'

One of Murdoch's men wriggled closer, keeping in the shadows. He winged a shot at Gil — and missed. Gil's Colts blazed in return and the man slumped in a heap. Jamie shouted to Murdoch:

'This is fool play — we can't get at them in the grave.'

Gil aimed for the sound of Jamie's voice; crimson streaks of flame spat back at him; shells whined past his head and furrowed the ground around him. Murdoch, well back out of range, gave another order:

'Rush them — concentrate on Palmer.'

There were shadowy movements and Gil's guns crashed fire. Keith's nerve broke; he grabbed the oilskin package and heaved it towards the sound of Murdoch's voice, calling, hysterically:

'Here's the message — now leave us alone!'

Gil swore and emptied his guns,
Alison's eyes blazed with anger as she
turned on her brother.

'You — you coward!'

Then she was reloading, pushing
guns into Gil's empty hands. But
Murdoch's men had had enough of the
fight. Murdoch had the message he
wanted; the girl could wait — and
Palmer. He called off his men and
made tracks.

Gil mounted the earth round the
grave. No shots came; he heard the
sound of horses' hoofs as their attackers
rode off. He helped Alison from the pit;
the girl's face was white with strain, but
her spirit was unbroken.

'Thanks, Gil. I must apologise for my
brother's weakness.'

Gil looked down at Keith Knox; the
youngster was leaning over the edge of
the grave, vomiting. The gunfight, on
top of uncovering Flint's corpse, had
been too much for his stomach. Gil
pulled him up and passed him to
Alison.

'Wait a little way off while I fill in the grave.'

He started shovelling the earth back, wondering if he could persuade Alison to let him ride for Paradise alone.

He sneaked a look at her as she waited, saw her red hair and the determined tilt of her chin, the obstinate light in her tawny eyes. He'd guessed they'd be riding for Paradise in the morning.

* ★ *

Beyond Sagebush the scenery was monotonous in its unchanging flatness, and the air was heavy with the sultry heat. The mountains seemed as far away as ever, rugged cliffs that shimmered in the haze of dust rising from the horses' hoofs.

Gil Palmer rode easily, relaxed in the saddle. The trail was clear and there was no chance of an ambush in such open country, though later on it would be different. His keen eyes had read the signs on the dusty trail; a bunch of riders had ridden towards Paradise within the last twelve hours. They could only be Murdoch's outfit — and already the hills made an undulating curve on the distant horizon. It would be different when they reached the hills; then, he'd have to ride with his eyes open and his guns ready for trouble.

He glanced sideways at Alison Knox. The girl was riding well, shoulders squared and head high, the line of her jaw revealing an inborn determination.

Gil smiled a little, thinking he'd never before met a girl like Alison; her beauty stirred his blood and her undaunted spirit roused his admiration.

His glance passed to Keith Knox. The youngster, mounted on the Indian pony, was hanging back, and he sat limply in the saddle. He hadn't wanted this journey to Paradise, with the near-certainty of a showdown with Murdoch, but he wouldn't desert his sister. Gil thought that was the only good thing he'd discovered about Keith Knox.

The horses made good time across the flatland, reaching the first line of foothills as the sun passed overhead. Gil was wary now, keeping off the main trail and riding between clumps of cedar and piñon trees, his eyes watchful for hidden snipers. A tiny creek wound between the hills and cattle watered in bunches. Farther on, Gil, riding in the lead, met two punchers. Both men were grim-faced and carried Winchesters at the ready.

The older man said: 'Stranger in these parts, I reckon?'

Gil nodded, studying the men carefully. They were lean and tanned and rode as if they were part of their mounts; the young man looked angry, as if he wanted to blast off with his rifle.

'Rustlers?' Gil asked lightly.

'Yeah.' The reply was bitter. 'We still got some beef left — and we aim to keep it!'

Alison and Keith joined them. Alison

asked: 'Trouble, Gil?'

'They think we're rustlers, after their cattle.'

The punchers took one look at Alison and lowered their guns. The younger one smiled at the girl.

'I don't reckon anyone will accuse you of stealing more than a man's heart,' he drawled. 'And that ain't agin the law!'

The older man said: 'Yuh figgering on going far? This is El Lobo's country — and no place for a girl.'

'We're heading for Paradise,' Gil replied. 'Was the reception for El Lobo? That hombre plaguing yuh?'

'Yeah, The Wolf's riding again. We lost a hundred head o' cattle, last week. And a rider — shot dead on night patrol.'

The older man looked at Gil. 'If you're looking for work, stranger, call in at the Twisted T ranch. You got the build of a useful man with a gun and Riley's hunting for good men, men who ain't afraid to stand and fight when El Lobo calls again.'

'We'll look in at the ranch,' Gil promised, 'but I ain't figgering on joining yore outfit.'

The younger puncher brooded. 'Paradise you say? You friends of that bunch who went through early this morning? Nine riders, one had his arm in a sling — the leader was wearing black, a granite-faced hombre with a pale face and intense black eyes.'

Gil smiled faintly. 'I don't reckon yuh'd call us friends exactly.'

He thought: Murdoch's outfit — he's packing a lot o' guns this trip. Nine men — one wounded. Aloud, he said: 'I guess we'll be riding. Luck with The Wolf!'

Alison and Keith followed as Gil left the valley through which the creek ran and followed the crest of the hills, avoiding wooded areas and keeping his eyes open. Though Murdoch had apparently ridden straight for Paradise, it was more than likely he'd leave a drygulcher to ambush them, and Gil didn't intend to be caught napping.

Over the second range of hills, the Twisted T ranch came into view. The bunkhouse was adobe, with corrals, bars and store sheds set in a circle round it, neatly filling the hollow between falling hills. The ground about had been cleared of trees, giving the ranchmen a clear view in case of attack. Most likely it had been built that way at the time of the Indian risings, but the lay-out would serve well if El Lobo raided the ranch.

Gil set the roan on a downward track. He drawled:

'We'll take a bite to eat with the Twisted T, and mebbe stay overnight. There's no sense in rushing into Paradise, with Murdoch expecting us. And the rancher may have news.'

He didn't amplify his last statement, for it was news of El Lobo that Gil was more interested in, and he didn't want that aspect of his trip to come into prominence. Alison and Keith swung down the slope without comment, and they came to the hard-baked patio before the house. As Gil tethered his horse, a stocky, grizzle-haired man came on to the porch; his right hand rested on the butt of a Colt six-shooter. He relaxed as he saw Alison, turned his head, and called into the house:

'Hi, Martha — we got visitors!'

He came across, introducing himself:

'I'm Tom Riley, owner of the Twisted T. You'll stay for a meal?'

'We were figgering on inviting ourselves, Mr Riley,' Gil grinned.

Martha, the rancher's wife, came out to greet them. She was a buxom, middle-aged woman, wiping the flour from her hands on an apron about her ample waist.

'Lordy!' she said. 'Visitors — and me up to my eyes in pastry-making — and me without a decent thing to wear when a pretty young lady comes a-calling — and . . . '

'I reckon,' said Gil easily, 'we'll jest mount our horses and ride around till yuh got the place ready for visiting royalty!'

'You'll do no such thing,' Martha Riley burst out. 'You'll come inside and rest while I rustle up some ham and eggs.'

Gil introduced Alison and Keith. Mrs Riley took the girl under her wing at once.

'What ever is such a pretty young thing as yourself doing in this rough neck of the country? And riding without a chaperone, too! Now, my dear, you must make yourself at home — you can use my room to tidy yourself up — and then you must tell me all about yourself and where you come from, and . . . '

Tom Riley smiled faintly as the two women disappeared into the house.

'It ain't often we see another woman out here,' he said.

The three men seated themselves in wicker chairs on the veranda of the house. Gil looked at Tom Riley, and drawled:

'Ran into a couple of yore boys down the trail. They said you're having a little trouble with rustlers, El Lobo.'

Riley's face darkened. 'A hundred head o' best beef rustled in a week — and one of my oldest riders shot down. And that ain't all. McBain over at Devil's Fork has been almost cleaned out. The Wells Fargo stage-coach was held up a couple o' weeks back; El Lobo's greasers murdered the driver and guard and got clear away with a load of gold bullion from the mine at Tinhorn. Then there was the raid on the bank at Fort Dunn, where The Wolf made off with the pay-roll for three outlying ranches. Yep, that renegade is causing a heap o' trouble around here.'

Keith Knox sneered: 'Don't you have a sheriff in this god-forsaken country? Back east these criminals would be hounded down and gaoled.'

Tom Riley fixed Keith with a grim stare.

'Son, back east ain't the same as the border. There ain't much law around these parts, except what a man makes at the point of a gun. A sheriff or two, with more guts than sense, have tried to take El Lobo — but that renegade has spies all along the border. It seems as if every Mexican this side o' the line is on his pay-roll — and those sheriffs aren't with us any more. You'll find 'em neatly lined up on Boot Hill.'

'I reckon there's little chance of locating El Lobo's bolt-hole and smoking him out?' Gil asked.

Riley laughed shortly. 'In the mountains? Not a chance. Not when the border's so close and he can jest slip across. Nope, The Wolf's a mighty smart hombre, but one day his luck is gonna run out.'

The conversation lagged. Gil looked up as Mrs Riley and Alison returned.

'Food,' said the rancher's wife. 'Come and get it!'

They trouped into the house and sat round a heavy cedar table. Gil's stomach felt suddenly empty at the smell of thick rashers of home-cured ham and fried eggs, and he ate heartily.

'Alison tells me you're going to Paradise, Mr Palmer,' Martha Riley said. 'Paradise is no town for a young girl; it's a rough place, and . . . '

Alison smiled: 'I'm sure I'll be all right with Gil — and my brother.' The last was an afterthought. Keith scowled, realising how little she relied on him now that Gil Palmer had joined them. Tom Riley stared shrewdly at Gil, noting the width of his shoulders, the well-used Colts and his air of self-confidence.

'I reckon Palmer is able to take care of himself,' he commented dryly, 'but with a gal it's different. You have to go to Paradise, Miss Knox?'

'I'm going,' Alison replied briefly.

Riley's expression was serious.

'Paradise is a gunman's town. All the roughnecks around the border hang out there, killers, cattle-thieves, hold-up men and the like — even El Lobo's men ride openly into the town. I'm telling yuh, Palmer, you'll have to look out for Miss Knox in Paradise.'

Gil smiled thinly, and said: 'I'll be looking.'

The meal over, Mrs Riley and Alison tended the washing-up. Riley asked: 'You'll stay the night, of course?'

'Good idea,' Keith snapped. 'I'm in favour of staying here — it wasn't my idea to go to Paradise, anyway.'

Riley went away to prepare rooms, leaving Gil and Keith on the veranda. The youngster didn't bother to answer when Gil said:

'I think I'll take a ride before bed. See you later.'

Gil urged his horse into the open, heading for the hills; beyond the ranch he travelled faster. The light wasn't going to last long, and he wanted to look around before dark, hoping to pick up a lead to El Lobo. No one could drive off a hundred head of cattle without leaving tracks, and Gil wanted to know which way The Wolf had gone.

From the veranda, Keith watched him ride away. Keith Knox had mixed feelings about Gil. He had a strong admiration for Gil Palmer's cool confidence and knowledge of the ways of the West; too, he had little doubt that Gil's guns would be all that stood between them and certain death if Alison persisted in going on with the search. Keith Knox kicked his heels, scowling — it wasn't his fault he'd been brought up in the east. If . . .

Alison joined him on the veranda, breaking into his chain of thought.

'Where's Gil?' she asked, puzzled at finding her brother alone.

Her tone annoyed Keith; these days, she seemed to think only of Gil Palmer — she might have been in love with him.

He said abruptly: 'Gone. He just got on his horse and rode off.'

'Oh!' Alison was taken aback. She felt hurt that Gil should ride off like that, without speaking to her.

Keith saw the flush come to her cheeks. He jeered:

'Did you really expect a gunman to have any decent feelings? You're a fool, sis — Palmer doesn't care about you. I doubt if we shall see Gil Palmer again — he's got cold feet and deserted you!'

Alison said: 'Don't be silly, Keith — of course Gil will be back.'

The evening shadows lengthened and the rancher's men rode in for the night, leaving only a two-man patrol to watch the cattle. Riley lit the oil-lamp and they sat round the table, talking. Still Gil did not return. Alison found herself wondering if he would . . .

The hour grew late. Mrs Riley rose to her feet and looked at Alison.

'I expect you're ready for bed, my dear?'

Alison hesitated, thinking of Gil, alone on the range.

'Stop worrying,' Riley advised. 'Palmer is one hombre able to look after himself.'

Keith sneered: 'I think we can forget Palmer — he isn't coming back, tonight or any other time. Perhaps you'll consider going back east now, Alison.'

The girl stood up, eyes glinting.

'I'm riding for Paradise in the morning,' she said calmly, 'whether Mr Palmer is here or not!'

She went upstairs to her room, leaving a strained quiet behind her. As she lay on her bed, waiting for sleep to come, she seemed to see the tall, sinewy figure of Gil Palmer and she cried a little because he had not come back.

3

Gil Palmer had forgotten about Murdoch and his outfit. The sun was a fiery red ball dropping towards the western hills as he toured the boundary of the Twisted T range. He saw no one, for Riley was keeping both cattle and men close to the ranch; only an occasional gopher disturbed the thorn and scrub underfoot.

Gil had found the tracks of a herd, heading away from the Twisted T, and was following it. The tracks were old, but plain, for many steers had passed that way, and he wasn't expecting trouble. The tracks passed through an arroyo formed by an overhang of rocks; a watercourse had flowed that way, but had now dried out. The dust was disturbed by the hooves of cattle and horses, and showed plainly, to Gil's expert eye, the herd which had passed by. It looked as if El Lobo was driving the cattle towards the mountains; maybe there was a pass over the border in that direction. What interested Gil most was that the general direction was that of Paradise.

Thinking of Paradise brought him back to Alison Knox. He frowned, remembering what Tom Riley had said about the town, and wondering what he could do to protect her.

Bothered by this problem, and intent on the tracks left by the stolen Twisted T herd, Gil was careless. He had forgotten Neil Murdoch and the possibility of an ambush — forgotten, too, that rattlesnakes made their home in the dry, rock-strewn beds of countless arroyos criss-crossing the cattle country of the southern states. So he was taken by surprise when his horse reared in the air, pawing with its forefeet as a rattler slithered across the path, hissing menacingly.

The shot boomed loudly, echoing through the arroyo. Gil felt the passage of the shell as it slammed into the roan's body. The horse shuddered under him, lurched heavily and plunged headlong, legs twisting under it. Gil rolled sideways out of the saddle, throwing himself clear, his right hand automatically grabbing a Colt.

He hit the ground with his shoulders, breaking his fall with his left hand, spitting out dust. The air was forced out of his lungs and he lay motionless, gasping, trying to watch for the snake and the man who had shot at him at the same time.

Gil gripped the Colt flat on the ground, waiting for a second shot and the tell-tale stab of red flame that would soon pin-point the ambusher. The rattlesnake, four feet of undulating death, hissed angrily as the horse's hooves threshed the air over its ugly, flattened head. It struck — and the roan shuddered out its last breath, then was still.

Sweat ran down Gil's face. He knew the shying horse had saved his life; that the drygulcher was an expert shot with a rifle. The shell would have struck him down if the roan had not reared in the air at the critical moment. So Gil lay still, feigning death. His Winchester was under the heavy body of the horse, out of reach — and a man with a Colt is no match for a rifleman.

The rattler slithered away from the horse, coiling its body, head swaying in the air, beady eyes fixed on Gil. Gil Palmer stared into the cruel eyes, his Colt trained on the ugly head; he could blast the snake before it struck — but his shot would warn the man hiding in the rocks. So Gil held his fire, sweating, a sickening sensation in the pit of his stomach. Man and snake stared at each other for long seconds — then the rattler turned away and he was alone with the dead horse.

Gil relaxed, his whole attention now transferred to the overhang of rock, searching for his ambusher. But the man was wary and did not reveal himself either by movement or sound.

Minutes passed, and the sun touched the horizon, its crimson rays streaking the arroyo with a bloody light. Gil forced himself to wait; soon the sun would set completely and a twilight, grey and uncertain, would cover him. If the would-be killer thought he were dead, he might come to rob the body; Gil smiled grimly, his trigger finger tightened at the thought. He waited.

The sun disappeared below the horizon and the light faded. Gil thought he heard the sound of a horse's hooves receding in the distance — but there might be more than one man lying up there with a rifle trained on him. Vultures gathered in the darkening sky, wheeling and soaring, waiting to come down to feed on the carcase. When the light was too bad for a rifleman to be sure of his aim, Gil rose to his feet. No shot followed, so he guessed the man had gone.

Gil pulled the dead body of his roan over to get at his Winchester. He checked the gun and set out to climb the rocks — he had to be sure the drygulcher wasn't still waiting. He soon found the place the ambusher had chosen to lie in wait; a niche high in the arroyo walls, screened by rocks. There were cigarette butts on the ground — and an empty rifle shell. Gill inspected it. The bullet which had buried itself in his roan had been fired from a Sharps rifle — he made a mental note of that fact, and resolved to find out which of Murdoch's men used a Sharps.

He found hoof marks leading towards Paradise and knew his man had flown. Gil considered his next move; he was twelve miles from the Twisted T, unmounted, and with night coming on. There seemed to be nothing for it but to start walking, so he returned to his dead horse and stripped off the saddle. He humped the saddle on his back and, with the Winchester in the crook of his arm, set off for the ranch. When he reached the end of the arroyo, he turned, and looked back; the vultures swooped, forming a black cloud over the carcase of the dead horse. Soon, Gil knew, there would be only white bones left — and those bones could easily have been his.

Evening shadows lengthened and night clouds gathered in the sky. Gil walked on, and the miles passed. A silver moon rose, bathing pine and cactus in its ghostly light. The saddle was heavy on his back and his thighs began to ache, for a westerner rarely walks; his high-heeled riding boots were crippling to walk in and, after an hour, he was cursing the man who had shot his horse.

The end of the second hour's walking brought him to a bunch of Riley's cattle, untended and grazing on the move. Gil's luck seemed out; he'd hoped to encounter one of the Twisted T riders and get a lift to the ranch, but Riley's men were way off with the main herd. He kept on walking.

The saddle became heavier, his legs

ached and his feet started to blister. Twice, he stopped to slake his thirst with the water canteen, hanging from his saddle. He wanted to rest, but decided against it. He felt he had to reach the ranch in case Alison needed him.

The moon was high and the time after midnight. A coyote howled from the timberline. Another hour passed and still he forced his weary limbs towards the Twisted T, following the line of the hills. He came across another bunch of steers; they lifted their heads to stare at him as he passed.

Gil could see the ranch buildings now, lightless and huddled together in the hollow, dark blotches in the moonlight. He quickened his pace as he moved down the slope to the patio; even his feet seemed less tired now that he was near Alison. The ranch was quiet and snores came from the punchers' bunkhouse. Gil smiled — everything was all right. Nothing had happened to the girl in his absence.

He dumped his saddle in the stables and entered the bunkhouse. There was an empty bed in the corner, that of one of the men on night patrol. Gil pulled off his boots, sighing with relief, and dropped flat on top of the blankets. His limbs felt like leaded weights trying to pull him through the blankets; his eyes closed and, in seconds, he was fast asleep.

⋆   ⋆   ⋆

Breakfast was on the table when Alison Knox came down the following morning. Tom Riley came in from the veranda.

'He's back,' the rancher said. 'Still sleeping — I guess he hasn't been back many hours.'

Alison's first feeling was one of relief; then she was annoyed with Gil. Why had he ridden off without a word? She began her breakfast, then Keith joined her.

'Look, Alison,' her brother said

abruptly. 'Now that Palmer's deserted us, I think we ought to go back east. You know what Riley said about Paradise.'

'I'm going on,' Alison replied calmly. 'But you can go back if you wish — Gil has returned in the night.'

'Oh!' Keith Knox looked disappointed; he didn't say any more. Tom and Martha Riley joined them at table and they finished breakfast. Gil came through the door a few minutes afterwards.

'Good morning, Mr Palmer,' Alison said.

Gil was surprised by the coolness of her tone; he nodded and sat down. There was a strained silence while Mrs Riley prepared Gil's breakfast, then Alison asked:

'Are you riding to Paradise with us, Mr Palmer?'

'Sure. I thought that was fixed?' Gil turned to Riley. 'I'll need a horse if you can fix me up. Mine was shot from under me, last night — I had to walk back.' He grinned wryly. 'My legs still ache — '

Alison's face went white and she half-rose in her seat. Her eyes searched him anxiously.

'You're not hurt, Gil?'

Her tone changed immediately; gone was the former coldness — now she was solicitous for his well-being. She was angry with herself for doubting him.

Gil sensed the change, and grinned.

'Only blistered feet,' he drawled. 'My horse took the lead.'

Riley's brows knitted. 'El Lobo?' he asked.

Gil shrugged. 'Maybe.' Riley saw he didn't want to talk about it.

'I've got a horse to spare — a bay. Large big-boned animal with plenty of stamina.'

'I'll take a look at it,' Gil said, and went out with the rancher.

The bay suited Gil and he saddled the horse. Alison joined him, not quite sure of herself.

'You're fit to ride, Gil? Or would you sooner rest today?'

'I'm fit enough — a little stiff, but an hour's riding will cure that.' He paused, looking into her tawny eyes, his face serious. 'There's another reason for pressing on right away. Murdoch probably thinks I'm dead and he's only got you and yore brother to deal with. I reckon he'll be a mite upset when I ride in with yuh — and the element of surprise is not to be despised when the odds are stacked against us.'

'It was Murdoch who — who shot at you?'

'Who else?' Gil shrugged his broad shoulders. 'One of Murdoch's men, I guess, left behind for that purpose.'

'I'm sorry, Gil — I misjudged you. Last night — ' Alison broke off, started again. 'I'm ashamed of myself for what I thought, and — and I'm glad you're riding with us.'

She turned and hurried back to the house. Gil stared after her, and his face creased in a faint grin. He followed her, more leisurely, after tightening the bay's cinch. He found Tom Riley with Keith and Alison.

'Leaving soon?' the rancher asked.

Gil nodded. 'Soon as I've made a few changes in Alison's dress. She sure is too conspicuous tricked out fancy-like. I reckon you can loan her some duds, leather pants and chaps, and a man's shirt. I want her to look less like a woman when we hit Paradise.'

Riley laughed. 'Sure thing, Palmer. I'll fit her out like a regular cowhand!'

Gil looked critically at Keith Knox.

'Same for the youngster. Some old clothes will make him look less like a tenderfoot — and maybe save a lot of trouble.'

Sulking, Keith took the outfit Riley brought and went to his room to change. Grinning, the rancher handed Alison the oldest, dirtiest pants and shirt he could dig up.

'I reckon no one will think she's the prettiest girl in the West with that outfit over her!'

When Alison had changed and appeared, self-consciously, Gil laughed.

'I guess you're right, Tom. She sure looks a hard-riding cuss!'

Even her brother smiled when he saw Alison in baggy leather pants with ragged chaps, a patched shirt too large for her, and her red hair hidden under a soiled bandanna. Riley fitted a tattered stetson over her head, calling:

'Martha — come and look at a regular bad hombre from the Rio Grande!'

Mrs Riley came in, gasped with astonishment. 'Lordy, whatever have you men done to the girl? She does look a sight, and no mistake — well, no one is going to take her for the beauty she is — and that's a good thing where you're taking her . . . '

Gil nodded, surveying Alison and her brother with satisfaction. His expression became serious.

'When we hit Paradise, Alison, remember to act like a man. And, Keith, we'll call her 'The Kid'. No sense in putting ideas into hombres' heads.'

He shook hands with the rancher and his wife, and Alison said her good-byes. The three of them went out to the stables, where the horses were saddled and waiting, and mounted. They swept out of the patio, past the corral and headed across the mesa, and the next stage on the treasure trail.

* * *

Whoever had named the town Paradise was a humorist. Wooden shacks sprawled higgledy-piggledy under a yawning hundred-foot bluff of ochreous clay, stretching to the edge of the desert, and stopping abruptly. The desert continued to the horizon, flat and drab and lifeless. Most of the shacks were windowless, some with doors hanging half off; dust and sand from the desert filtered into every crack, piling up in corners, drifting lazily across the bare, unboarded streets. The air had a harsh, grey light and even the sun only served to accentuate the waterless waste encroaching over the edge of the town.

Years back a gold strike had caused Paradise to come into being. But the gold seam had run out, and Paradise — bitterly cursed by the men it had tricked — was left to itself. It became a ghost town, silent and deserted with only disused workings, an occasional spade stuck crookedly in the sand, and a skeleton to mark the place where men had once hoped to strike a fortune.

Then the outlaws had come. Driven west by the lawmen, tough hombres had drifted into Paradise, and stopped to make the town their own. A saloon had opened, a store opposite, a few shacks about them housed sullen men with quick-firing guns. Paradise had no use for a sheriff; the stage never stopped there, and honest men avoided the place. The saloon was the centre of the town — and Boot Hill the end.

Gil, Alison and Keith came into

Paradise from the east, after sundown. Lights gleamed yellowly from the saloon, and the sound of men drinking and cursing thinned to ghostly whisperings on the edge of the town. Shots rang out, echoing sharply in the still air — there was silence for a moment, then the drinking began again.

Alison's face was composed and she was sure of herself; Keith was uneasy, and moistened his lips with the tip of his tongue.

'Nothing to fret about,' Gil said easily. 'Shooting's the usual music around here. Just keep to yourself and let me handle anyone who starts trouble.'

He reined in his bay before they reached the saloon, and dismounted, looping the reins to a hitching rack. A wooden shack stood a little way back from the dusty path; it had boarded-up windows and a door that swung on one hinge. Gil took a look inside, found it untenanted, and announced:

'We'll use this for tonight. Alison, see

about a meal; Keith build a fire — I'll see to the horses.'

Behind the bare shed, a corrugated iron roof supported by worm-eaten timbers formed a stable. Gil unharnessed the horses and fed and watered them; returning to the shack, he found they had a visitor. The newcomer leaned on the door frame and poured out a stream of questions.

'Say, you younkers don't look the usual Paradise type — you hiding out from the law? I had a raw kid come in a few months back, chased by a posse — had a bullet in his lung, but I patched him up all right. You wounded? No? Maybe you left someone down the trail in need of my services? Let me introduce myself — I'm the doc around here — the only sawbones for miles. Hombres call me Doc Paradise and I'm telling yuh, if you get lead poisonin', I'm the man to see . . . '

Gil said: 'We don't aim to get shot up, Doc, so we won't bother yuh none.'

Doc Paradise swung round. He was

an old man with a shock of white hair and sharp eyes; his clothes were stained with egg yolk and tobacco juice. He looked like a man who had known better days — a long time back.

'Waal, stranger,' he said, 'those are mighty fine sentiments, but let me tell you, Paradise is a tough town. I see gunfights start over nothing a-tall.' He shook his white head.

Gil touched his gun-butts significantly.

'In that case,' he drawled, 'maybe I'll give you some work, Doc.'

Doc Paradise grinned and slapped his thigh.

'How about a business proposition? You shoot 'em up and I cure 'em — we split the doctoring fees fifty-fifty — Is it a deal?'

Gil laughed. 'Sorry, Doc. I'm a peace-loving hombre and don't hold with shooting.'

'No? Waal, you won't be long in Paradise before yuh have to draw your irons in self-defence. I only hope it ain't you I have to dig the lead out of — you staying long? Maybe you'll buy me a drink for good luck? I didn't catch your name — '

Gil shook his head. 'I didn't say — and we're just riding through.' He tossed a silver dollar in the air. 'Here, buy yourself a drink and don't bother us any more.'

Doc caught the coin. He turned and headed for the saloon, calling after him:

'Thanks, stranger. I'll take this on account — in case yuh get shot up afore yuh leaves town.'

Gil grimaced. 'I guess it won't be long before every hombre in Paradise knows we're here. Let's eat before we get more visitors.'

Alison had prepared a meal of bacon and beans, with coffee to follow. They sat down and started to eat.

'It's a shame about the doctor,' Alison said. 'Do you suppose there's anything we can do to help him? He must have been used to better things than this.'

Gil shook his head. 'The doc's a long way gone. Probably he slipped the wrong side of the law one day and had to ride. After that, his only way of earning money would be taking slugs out of rustlers. And he drinks too much; his breath knocked me sideways.'

'Let's find grandfather's clue and get out of this hole,' Keith said irritably. 'Forget about that old fool.'

Alison snapped: 'Shut up, Keith!'

Keith glowered and lapsed into silence. After a while, Gil said:

'I'm going to take a look round town and see what I can find out. You two stay here and keep out of trouble. I shan't be long.'

Remembering Sagebush, Gil headed straight for the cemetery, but he was disappointed. Half the graves were without names or markers, and he found no indication that one of Seth Knox's party might lie buried there. He retraced his steps, thinking hard. It was certain that Knox would not have trusted any of Paradise's usual inhabitants with a message.

Walking the dark streets lined with dingy shacks, it occurred to Gil that Knox's party must have used one of the tumbledown huts, just as he was doing. The clue must be in that hut, probably under the floorboards. But how could he find out which shack the party had used five years ago?

He reached the saloon, yellow light streaming out through dirty windows, the raucous voices of men far gone in drink echoing curses. Murdoch might have already located the message and gone on; he'd know for sure if none of Murdoch's outfit were drinking in the bar.

Inside, the air was thick with tobacco smoke. A single oil lamp hanging from a rafter gave insufficient light for the size of the room. Immediately under the lamp, card players sat round a rickety table. Swarthy-faced Mexicans outnumbered white men by two to one at the bar; bullet holes decorated the walls and floor and the sawdust reeked of spilled alcohol. Gil saw Doc Paradise propped against the counter, steadily emptying a bottle of whisky — and Murdoch, with Jamie Riggs.

They were not alone; two other men sat at their table in the corner, drinking and talking. Gil looked them over. One was a giant of a man with red jowls and a stubbled jaw; the other was thin and angular with a lean, tanned face. Both of them wore two Colts apiece and they looked what they were — hired killers.

Murdoch hadn't noticed Gil and he was about to slip outside, back to Alison and Keith, when Doc Paradise let out a greeting:

'Hi, stranger, take a drink with me. Boys, this hombre just hit Paradise and he's a right — '

The men at the bar passed Gil a glance, then ignored him. Murdoch's head turned, he started and came to his feet.

'Tex — you fool! You've muffed it.'

Gil pushed Doc aside and faced Murdoch.

'Stand back, Doc,' he said gently. 'There may be business coming yore way.'

Tex stood up slowly, and on his red face was a strained expression, as if he were looking at a ghost. Gil had no doubt in his mind that this was the man who had drygulched him and shot his horse.

'If you're the expert with a Sharps,' Gil said deliberately, 'I guess you're the hombre I'm looking for.'

Mexicans scattered, leaving Gil alone in the centre of the bar. Tex's face gradually assumed its natural colour; he stepped forward, hands over the butts of his guns. With Slim and Jamie to back his play, he felt confident he could finish the job he'd set out to do in the arroyo. Gil stood still, icy calm, his arms hanging loose at his sides, feet slightly apart. He could kill Tex in a straight draw — but there were the others to reckon with. He decided on a bluff.

No one saw his arms move. With

incredible speed, he drew his .45s, directing the muzzles at the group about the table. It seemed as if, one moment, he was relaxed and smiling; the next as if his guns appeared out of nowhere, his face cold. A gasp of disbelief sighed through the room.

Tex froze, the blood draining from his face. He realised that Gil could have shot him down before he reached the butts of his own guns.

Gil said: 'I'm giving yuh till sunrise to get out of town, Tex — then I'm coming after yuh. That's fair warning.'

Slim and Jamie made no move to draw; their faces were tensed, waiting for the next move. Murdoch walked forward, his dark eyes glittering, a smouldering cheroot clenched between his teeth.

'You've got the luck of ten devils, Palmer,' he gritted. 'But don't think you'll get away with this. You were a fool to come to Paradise, a fool to side with the girl.'

The tension eased through the room.

Men began drinking again. Doc Paradise mumbled:

'Shoot 'em down, fellar — fifty-fifty, like I said. I ain't no welsher.'

He staggered a little under the influence of whisky, and Gil pushed him aside again. Murdoch said, fixing his eyes on Gil:

'She in town, Palmer?'

Gil ignored the question, holstered his guns and made for the door. He paused at the batwings:

'Keep your Sharps expert out o' my way, Murdoch — and the same applies to you.'

He ducked through the door and went out into the darkness. No shots followed him; Tex hadn't got over the speed of his draw yet. Gil was turning away from the saloon when a Mexican passed him, on his way to the bar. The Mex was tall and lean, dark-skinned with a hooked nose. Gil stopped walking, half-turned to get a good look at the man — and saw a living scar down the left side of his face, the memento of a knife-thrust which had taken off half his ear.

Gil stopped breathing; his pulse beat faster. This creature was Velasquez, El Lobo's right-hand. Velasquez took no notice of Gil and passed into the saloon; he was sleek and smooth, with the build of a panther, and dressed in a gaudy shirt and neckerchief, with fringed and decorated chaparejos. His sombrero was laced with blue and red beads and his guns inlaid with ivory and silver. He walked with an exaggerated swagger.

Gil ducked into the shadows and crept round the side of the saloon till he found a window that allowed him a view of what was going on inside. He saw Murdoch leave with Tex and the slim man; Jamie stayed at the bar, drinking. Velasquez went straight to the counter and started talking in Spanish to the barman. Although Gil could hear what was said, his knowledge of Spanish was not good enough for him to follow the conversation, but from the gestures and looks passed at Jamie, Gil guessed that Velasquez was asking about the strangers in town.

Velasquez moved across to Jamie and pushed a drink towards him, smiling and showing pearly white teeth.

'Welcome to Paradise, señor. You weel drink with me?'

Jamie grabbed the glass. 'Sure I will.'

Velasquez guided Jamie to a corner seat and they sat down, drinking and smoking. Gil passed on to the next window, nearer the table; there was a knothole below the sash and he could hear perfectly through this. Jamie's breath was heavy and his hand unsteady; his voice slurred a little, revealing he'd been drinking for some hours.

'Here's to yuh, Mex!'

Velasquez sipped his drink slowly, plying Jamie with liquor. He was a cat playing with the mouse.

'You are with Señor Murdoch?'

Jamie boasted: 'Me and him are partners.'

'Señor Murdoch comes from El Grande? He ees a big man there. I wonder, now, why it ees he bothers to come to Paradise?'

Jamie grinned in the Mexican's face. 'That's a secret — I ain't telling you. No sir, Jamie Riggs can keep a secret!'

Velasquez showed his teeth in a flashy smile.

'Perhaps it ees the Señor Murdoch does not take you into his confidence?'

'By grab, yuh got it wrong, Mex.' Jamie snorted in disgust. 'I'm telling yuh, it was me as took him into my confidence. If it hadn't been for me, Murdoch would never have heard of the Indian gold, no sir. I took him in partnership — I'm the boss o' this outfit.'

The Mexican's eyes gleamed with interest. 'Gold, Señor Riggs? In Paradise?' He laughed. 'No, the señor is joking with me.'

Jamie hunched over the table, lowering his voice.

'Not here.' He waved his hand about

vaguely. 'Somewhere around — perhaps in the mountains. We're following up a trail — there's clues — '

Velasquez's face revealed nothing. He might have been thinking: how much truth is there in the words of this drunken gringo?

Aloud, he said: 'I know the mountains well. This Murdoch, he ees not a man to be trusted. Now, perhaps — we can make a deal, Señor Riggs?'

Jamie shook his head, sniggering.

'No deal, Mex. I ain't cutting no one else in on this trip.'

Velasquez rose to his feet, still smiling.

'Perhaps you weel change your mind, señor, if this Murdoch double-crosses you. Remember me, in that moment. I think we shall meet again — and perhaps, then, you weel tell me more of this gold you seek. Adios!'

He left the table and walked through the batwing doors of the saloon, out into the night. Gil moved through the shadows and watched the Mexican mount and ride off. Soon El Lobo would hear of the treasure hunt — and come to see what it was all about. Gil Palmer smiled grimly; it looked as if he wouldn't have to hunt his man after all — The Wolf would come to him.

He moved quickly through the dark streets, towards the shack where Alison and Keith waited. Tomorrow, he thought, would bring a new threat to the girl he had sworn to protect.

★　★　★

Gil was up early the next morning, before many of the inhabitants of Paradise were astir. He moved from hut to hut, searching for a clue that would indicate where Seth Knox and his party had stayed five years before. He knew it was a hopeless quest, but he kept on, till he had covered all the shacks that were not occupied. The others were going to be more difficult.

He back-tracked, heading for the breakfast Alison was preparing, and met Doc Paradise. The old man was leaning over a hitching rack, eyeing Main Street with a critical eye.

'Ain't seen no sign of him yet,' Doc said.

Gil stopped. 'Who?'

'Why, that Tex fellar. You figure he's cut and run? I was hoping he'd make a stand and you'd shoot him up a bit. I can use the business.'

'You bloodthirsty old rogue!' Gil flipped the old man a fifty-cent piece. 'Go oil your throat and forget about shooting up your clients.'

Gil was turning away when a thought came into his head. Doc Paradise had been around a long time — and he had more curiosity than a cat. It was almost certain he'd remember Seth Knox.

'Wait a minute, Doc. There's something I want to know. Do you — '

He broke off suddenly as his eye caught sight of a black-suited figure, smoking a cheroot and heading for the shack where Alison and Keith were hiding out. Neil Murdoch was alone, walking with a purposeful stride.

Doc Paradise said: 'I reckon I know most of what goes on around here, and for a consideration — '

'Later,' Gil said over his shoulder, moving after Murdoch.

The gambler was apparently unaware of Gil; he reached the door of the shack and pushed it open and went in. Gil came up fast and quietly, hitching his guns for action. Murdoch's move puzzled him. If the gambler intended to start anything, where were his gunmen? Gil waited outside the door, watching and listening.

'Miss Knox?' Murdoch called. 'Hallo there — '

His voice died away as he saw two derelict-looking figures appear. For a moment their disguises tricked him, then he recognised them. He chuckled.

'Smart of Palmer to dress you up like a couple of cowhands,' he said. 'But you're too lovely to hide like that, Alison — I'd know you anywhere.'

Keith had pulled a gun on Murdoch.

103

'Get out!' he said, his face white and tensed.

The gambler smiled: 'What's the hurry? I've a proposition to put. Now, Miss Knox, I realise I haven't appeared in a good light so far, but I'm not the bad man I appear. Why not listen to what I have to say?'

Alison faced him fearlessly, a little puzzled.

'What do you want? I'm not forgetting your men tried to murder us at Sagebush.'

'Murder? I admit I wanted to — er — eliminate — Palmer, but I assure you my men had the strictest orders not to harm you in any way. I have the deepest regard for you, Miss Knox, the very deepest. The affair at Sagebush was unfortunate, but I acted without thinking. Now, I have thought it over — and I want you to trust me — '

'I'd sooner,' the girl said coolly, 'trust a snake!'

Murdoch's night-black eyes glittered. 'That was unwise of you, Alison. You're alone in the roughest town in the West. Palmer can't help you — he's only one man. Now, we're both after the same thing — the treasure left by the Aztecs. Why not throw in with me? You'll get a fair share, and protection from El Lobo. What do you say?'

'No,' Alison said shortly. 'And I'd advise you to leave before Gil gets back.'

'So Palmer's not here?' Murdoch's sudden movement took Keith by surprise. Murdoch stepped forward and knocked the gun from the youngster's hand; his fist came up in a short jab to Keith's jaw and the kid went over backwards, slamming his head against the wall. He slumped to the floor, stunned.

Murdoch made a grab for Alison. 'You're a beauty, my girl — and I'm going to have you, whether you like it or not!'

Gil came through the door like a whirlwind, seized Murdoch by the collar and broke his grip on the girl. He flung the gambler against the wooden wall of the shack and stood over him, eyes blazing, hands on the butts of his Colts.

'Go for yore gun, Murdoch — I'm going to kill yuh for that!'

Murdoch staggered upright, panting for air. 'Damn you, Palmer,' he snarled. 'Go ahead and shoot — you know I'm no match for you.'

Alison broke the tense silence.

'Let him go, Gil — don't shoot!'

There was a note of horror in her voice, as if she knew he would murder the man who had molested her if she didn't stop him. The tension eased inside Gil; he relaxed, but did not take his eyes from Murdoch's face.

'Draw yore gun — and throw it away.'

The gambler hesitated; then his hand went under his coat, closed round the butt of his Colt. He remembered Gil's lightning draw in the saloon, and his courage wavered. He drew his gun from its holster and threw it from him. It clattered noisily on the bare wooden boards.

'What now, Palmer?'

'Alison,' Gil said, 'get his gun and keep guard. I'd sure hate to be disturbed for the next few minutes.'

When she had picked up the Colt, Gil unfastened his gun-belt and let it drop.

'All right, Murdoch, put up yore dukes — I'm going to knock hell out of yuh for touching Alison.'

Murdoch thought he'd catch Gil by surprise; he sprang forward, arms flailing. He was a big man, powerful, and not used to giving in to anybody; he hurled himself at Gil, trying to get his arms round him. Gil slammed wicked punches into Murdoch's belly, winding him; he followed up with a right to the jaw and a left that brought a red weal to the gambler's pale cheek. Murdoch dropped, grabbed Gil's groin as he fell, then they were rolling on the floor, grunting, and punching short jabs to each other's body.

Gil threw Murdoch away from him and got to his feet; he waited for Murdoch to rise, then started in again, smashing a left to Murdoch's eye; again and again he hammered the eye till it puffed up, purpling — Murdoch went to the wall, sagging, hardly able to see. He began to slide down the wall, his face a bloody pulp, his hair over his eyes, his clothes dusty and torn. Gil grabbed Murdoch by the collar, swung him over his head and flung him through the door.

The gambler landed in a heap in the dust and lay still. After a while, he got up and limped off. His voice shook with rage.

'I'll get you, Palmer! I'll get you — don't think you can handle Neil Murdoch and get away with it!'

Gil laughed. 'Bring yore gunmen with yuh — I'll take care of them, too. And if I find you within a hundred feet of Miss Knox again I'll fill yuh plumb full o' lead. Get going!'

Murdoch disappeared down Main

Street, dabbing at his face with a handkerchief; it was going to be a long time before he felt like making a public appearance.

Doc Paradise wandered up, grinning and rubbing his hands.

'That was a dandy fight, Palmer, just dandy. I reckon you handled him a treat. Say, you figure he'd appreciate medical aid?'

'I reckon not,' Gil said. 'If I was you, Doc, I'd give Murdoch a wide berth till he's recovered his temper.'

Doc's face fell. 'Maybe you're right. Say, you wanted to know some little thing . . . is there a couple o' dollars in it? I could sure use a drink right now.'

'Yeah, come in and take breakfast with us, Doc.'

'You're not hurt, Gil?' Alison looked at him anxiously.

'Murdoch's the one as got hurt.'

'Serve the swine right!' Keith Knox snapped. He had recovered from Murdoch's blow, though he had a nasty bump on the back of his head.

Gil ducked his head in a bucket of cold water and rubbed his face dry; he belted on his guns. 'I'm sure ready for breakfast, Alison.'

She served it up hot, bacon and fried potatoes, with thick slices of bread, and the four of them sat down to eat. Black coffee followed, and Doc Paradise made a wry face.

'Leave me out,' he said. 'That stuff ain't food for my hang-over.'

He looked at Alison in a thoughtful way. 'You know, you remind me of someone. There's something about the set of your jaw — and those eyes. Yep, I remember now. Fellar called Knox passed this way — say, that must be four or five years back now. Strange how yuh remind me of him.'

'This Knox,' Gil said lazily, 'did he stay in town?'

'No, sir. Came with two other hombres, stocked up with provisions and left town before daybreak. Never did figure what they was doing out this way.'

'I supposed Knox stayed in one of these shacks? It would be an odd coincidence if it was this one — I mean, with Alison looking so much like him.'

'Not this here shack,' Doc Paradise said, chewing a quid of tobacco. 'They used the old Stevens place, the other side of town — only shack in town with a red brick chimney. I must say it looked odd, a wooden shack with a red brick chimney sticking up from it.'

Gil knitted his brows. He'd been all over Paradise, but he couldn't recall seeing a building answering to that description.

'Whereabout did you say this shack was?'

''Tain't there now — burnt to the ground, couple o' years back. That was a night, that was. Black Pete was liquored up and shootin' off his guns all over the place. One of the Warder brothers hit him over the head with a bottle and they slung him in the shack to cool off — but I guess he wasn't out, nor sober neither. Must have tried to light a quirly, for, an hour later the place was afire. Wasn't nothing anyone could do about it. Being of wood, the shack burnt down in no time at all. Black Pete never got a burial either, cause there was only ashes — not a stick left. I reckon you'd have a job to find where it had been even.'

Gil thought bitterly: so that's the end of the trail. Seth Knox's clue would be destroyed with the hut . . .

Alison leaned forward eagerly. 'But you know which way they went from here? Which direction they took?'

'Sure,' Doc Paradise said. 'Across the desert. Mad if you ask me. No one would get me out there — nothing but sand, no water, nothing. Say, you ain't a-figgering to follow them?'

Gil said quickly: 'Of course not.'

Doc brooded: 'Can't imagine why anyone should want to head into the desert. Even if they reached the other side — which ain't likely — there's only mountains. And some say El Lobo hides out there.' He shook his shock of white hair. 'No, sir, you wouldn't get me to set foot across that desert.'

He fixed his eyes on Gil.

'There was something yuh wanted to know, Palmer. Just spill it, and — '

'I reckon it wasn't anything important. Plumb gone out o' my head.'

He tossed a coin in the air, and Doc caught it.

'I guess the saloon will be open by now,' Gil said casually.

Doc Paradise grinned, spat a stream of tobacco juice through the door and followed it into the street.

'I'd advise yuh to forget about that desert, Palmer. Knox and his buddies never came back . . . ' He disappeared up the street, heading for the saloon.

Keith said: 'Well, that's that. Now we can go back east. Even Alison isn't stubborn enough to consider crossing a desert.'

'That's where you're wrong!' The girl stuck out her chin determinedly. 'I'm going on; Gil, you'll come with me, won't you?'

Gil said: 'I think your brother's right, Alison. The desert's no place for a girl. I suggest you return east and leave me to carry on; I'll follow up the trail for yuh.'

'No! I appreciate your offer, Gil — but I'm crossing the desert. I'm determined to find out what happened to grandfather. Keith can turn back if he wishes, but I'm not. And I hope you'll come with me, Gil.'

Gil gave a faint sigh. He could see it was no use arguing with her — and El Lobo was somewhere in the mountains beyond the desert.

'All right,' he said, 'I guess I'm coming with yuh.'

4

Slim opened his eyes wide as Murdoch entered the shack, his face marked, one eye swollen.

'Thunder! What hit yuh, boss?'

'Palmer,' Murdoch gritted. 'I'll scatter that cowpuncher half across Texas before I'm through with him.'

He dipped a towel in a basin of water and bathed his wounds, wincing as the icy water stung his face. Slim leaned against the wall, watching. He said:

'How far do yuh trust that Jamie hombre?'

Murdoch looked up. 'What do you mean by that?'

'Only that he got drunk last night — and talked to a Mex — Velasquez, El Lobo's right-hand gun!'

'The — fool! I haven't enough trouble on my hands without him opening his mouth. I'll fix him! Give me a gun, Slim.'

He grabbed the Colt Slim handed him and stalked to the next shack, where Jamie was sleeping off his stupor. Jamie was flat out, snoring between blankets stretched out on the floor. He was fully dressed except for his boots. Murdoch pulled the blankets from Jamie's face and kicked him in the ribs.

'Get up!' he snarled savagely.

Jamie gave a yelp and rolled clear of the blankets, staggering to his feet. He flared at Murdoch. 'What's the idea?'

Murdoch said: 'I've warned you to keep sober, but no, you can't stay away from hard liquor — so you open your mouth and blab my business to a Mexican. You — fool!'

Jamie protested: 'I didn't tell him anything.'

'No? D'you happen to know who it was you were talking to? Velasquez! El Lobo's first lieutenant! And how long do you think it will take The Wolf to get on our trail now that you've told him about the treasure?'

Jamie licked his lips. Murdoch had a gun in his hand and Slim stood in the doorway — his own guns were on the wall, out of reach.

'I didn't spill anything,' he whined.

'Shut up!' Murdoch grated.

He was feeling sore over taking a beating from Gil, and wanted someone to relieve his feelings on. Murdoch stepped in, eyes blazing, lips drawn back. He raised his arm and struck Jamie across the face with the barrel of his gun; the foresight raked a groove in his cheek and blood ran down. Jamie crashed backwards into the wall and Murdoch went after him, pistol-whipping him with the Colt's barrel.

Jamie howled, covering his bleeding face with his hands. 'Slim — pull him off!'

But Slim only grinned and rolled himself a cigarette. He had no sympathy.

Murdoch was a head taller than Jamie, and took full advantage of his height; he cornered the gunman, his granite face a mask of rage, hitting him again and again with the gun, imagining it was Gil Palmer he had at his mercy.

Blindly, Jamie groped for his guns hanging on the wall, trying to protect his face with his arms. Murdoch reversed the gun in his hand and crashed down the butt on Jamie's skull; the gunman dropped like a log — he was out cold.

Panting, Murdoch stood back; he tossed the Colt away from him and strode out into the street. He stopped to light a fresh cheroot, puffed at it, then walked on. Neil Murdoch felt a lot better. Slim watched him go, then sauntered away to join in the search for Seth Knox's clue.

It was minutes before Jamie stirred. He moaned as he recovered consciousness, crawled to his knees and pulled himself upright. He cleaned his face, swearing with pain. He looked in the mirror, and shuddered. Murdoch wasn't getting away with this . . .

He belted on his guns and rolled his

blankets, then slipped out the back way. He felt he needed a drink more than at any time in his life, but he didn't go near the saloon; he saddled his gelding and headed out of town — but he wasn't going far.

The words of Velasquez echoed through his head: 'Perhaps you weel change your mind . . . when Murdoch double-crosses you!'

Jamie Riggs headed for the hills behind the bluff, seeking a hideout. Sooner or later, he would meet Velasquez — and the Mexican would lead him to El Lobo. Jamie was changing sides; he'd cut The Wolf in on the Indian treasure — and El Lobo would take care of Murdoch.

★ ★ ★

'Sand!' said Keith Knox bitterly. 'Nothing but sand!'

The desert stretched to the horizon and beyond; the mountains seemed to move in the shifting haze, receding to infinity, wavering like a mirage. The sand under the horses' hooves was soft and loose, eddying in dust clouds, covering the riders in a fine powder. The heat of the sun beat down on them with relentless fury.

Keith pulled the cork from his water canteen and drank thirstily.

'Take it easy,' Gil warned. 'There's no waterholes out here.'

Keith scowled and replaced the cork in his bottle. His throat felt parched, the clothes were stiff and scorched on him and he'd never been so hot in his life. There was no shade. Behind them, Paradise was a flickering image in the bleached yellow sand.

Gil watched Alison anxiously, but she seemed to be bearing the heat well enough. She sat stiffly in the saddle of her Indian pony, lips set in a firm line, her eyes fixed on the mountains in the distance. He glanced back, shielding his eyes from the bright sunlight, watching for Murdoch's riders. But the horizon was unbroken; either Murdoch had not yet discovered their absence, or he was having difficulty persuading his men to attempt the desert crossing.

Gil mopped the sweat from his face and frowned at the trail of hoof prints they were leaving behind them; in the sand, nothing could be done about that — but Murdoch would have no difficulty in following, once he set out.

All day they rode without stopping, then as night clouds gathered and the sun dropped from view, he called a halt.

'Rest the horses, and they get first call on the water. We'll ride again as soon as the moon comes up. I don't aim to be stuck out here longer than necessary.'

Neither Keith nor Alison felt like eating; they rinsed out their mouths with water and sat on their saddles, stripped off the ponies. Gil smoked a cigarette. No one felt like talking; even Keith had given up complaining.

It was suddenly dark and a breeze stirred the sand, rippling it gently. A star twinkled, then another; the moon came out, a silver disc in a cloudless sky, illuming the desert with a cold light.

'Saddle up,' Gil said, rising.

They started off again. The mountains were silver peaks, far away. It seemed as if they would never get out of that sandy waste, never see green grass or leafy trees again. The desert was harsh and forbidding in the moonlight, and the bones of a steer protruded from the sand, ghastly white. Alison shuddered as they passed the grim relic.

The horses could only travel at walking pace in the soft sand. Gil took the lead, setting the pace, and Keith and Alison followed. The night hours wore on and a coldness settled over the desert. The desert was a land of extremes, hot by day, cold by night. Gil knew that the heat of the next day would seem worse by contrast.

They stopped, wrapped blankets about them, and rode on again. They crossed a line of dunes, and the ground dropped abruptly; a wide arroyo crossed the desert, the bed of a river which had long since dried up. Gil let his mount find its own way down the steep bank and up the other side; not even a cactus plant grew where once a mighty river had tumbled foaming waters. It seemed as if life was a blasphemy in such a place.

Presently they came upon the bleached bones of a horse, terrifying reminder of what could happen if they failed to reach the mountains; of the rider, there was no sign. The ponies shied at the half-buried skeleton, whinnying pitifully.

Keith started to whine. 'Let's turn back, Alison. We'll never cross this desert.' His lips were cracked and the words came out thickly. 'We'll die! Let's turn back.'

'Stop it!' Alison snapped.

Gil said nothing. He kept the bay's head to the distant mountain peaks, silently admiring the girl, an easterner unused to roughing it. Yet not a word of complaint came from her lips.

The sun peeped over the horizon, edging the desert with garish light, and still the mountains seemed no nearer. Gil called another halt. They rested the horses and packed their blankets; ate a little, washing the dry crumbs down with sips of precious water. They still had a long way to go, and no chance of refilling their canteens.

The sun's rays were hazing the air when they set off again. Gil's bay had plenty of stamina, but the Indian ponies were tiring; the pace slackened, the drifts of sand seemed to be deeper, more treacherous underfoot. The sun climbed high and the sky turned bright blue, hurtful to the eyes, cloudless; the reflected flare of the sun off the bleached sand was a thousand stabbing daggers of crystal.

Noon, with a ball of fire over their heads, beating down waves of intense heat; the harsh glare throbbing through shifting layers of misty air. Keith slumped in the saddle, eyes glazed, muttering to himself in a toneless voice;

124

a fringe of beard glistened with perspiration on his chin, and his face was white despite the sun. Even Alison had lost some of her poise; her jaw still revealed determination, but the light had gone out of her tawny eyes; she was listless, without energy.

Gil said: 'I'd give a lot for a thunderstorm, right now.'

Alison forced a smile. Keith didn't seem to have heard; he was cracking up fast, Gil thought. And the hot sky showed no sign of a cloud; rain was as remote as the chance of an honest sheriff in Paradise. They rode on in silence, and presently came on another pile of bones. Alison shuddered, and looked away. Keith didn't seem to see them at all. Gil reined in his horse and stared down at the skeleton; no horse or steer this, but a man — a man laid out in a straight line, his arms pointing to the mountains ahead.

Gil licked his dry lips so that he could speak.

'Looks like Seth Knox left a signpost.

I reckon this poor galoot must be either Cassidy or Harper, and that would be his horse we passed, way back.'

'It's horrible,' the girl said, her voice quivering.

'Waal,' Gil drawled, 'we know now that we're on your grandfather's trail.' He shielded his eyes and stared across the sandy waste to the line of mountains flickering in the heat haze. 'All we have to do is keep going.'

They left the skeleton signpost behind, following the direction of its pointing arm. The sun beat down with increasing heat and the horses lagged, tongues hanging out, sweat glistening on their hides. Gil's clothes stuck to his skin and the saddle under him felt red-hot; desert dust rose in clouds from the bay's hooves, filtering through the neckerchief over his mouth and nose, choking him with its bitter, alkaline taste. He felt as if he were being slowly roasted in an oven.

Late afternoon revealed a vulture in the sky. Gil squinted through the haze and commented:

'Likely there's a water-hole near, but don't hope too much. It'll be mud, and poisoned mud at that. Still, we're a lot nearer the mountains. I reckon we should be out of this desert tonight.'

The horses seemed to smell water; they moved quicker, raising their heads, sniffing. Keith came back to life; his eyes gleamed and a terrible voice came out of his parched throat.

'Water — water!'

The horses were stumbling forward in eagerness to quench their thirst. Gil held his bay in check, called sharply:

'Don't give them their heads. Don't let them drink — unless yuh want to walk the rest of the way.'

The water-hole was a dirty depression in the sand. There were bones scattered round it, heaped up, and the dry mud showed hoofprints, set solid. There was no water visible, and the place stank. The ponies didn't want to go on; they milled around, restless, sensing that there should be water near.

Keith fell out of his saddle and staggered, in a drunken line, to the water-hole. He slumped to his knees, dug madly at the caked mud with his hands. His eyes burned feverishly, and his voice was a cracked scream echoing across the desert.

'Water! I've got to have water!'

Alison looked on, horrified.

'Keith! Don't drink — '

Gil swung out of his saddle with a curse. He reached Keith, grabbed him by the collar and dragged him upright. The youngster struggled, wanting to get at the water; he fought with the strength of a madman. Gil knew there was no use arguing with him; he drew back his arm and slung a sledgehammer punch to the boy's jaw. Keith Knox dropped like a felled tree.

'Sorry, Alison,' Gil said. 'There was no other way. Keep the horses clear of the water-hole. I'll look after your brother.'

He brought the bay to its haunches and carried Keith to the shade cast by the horse. The youngster's water-bottle was empty; Gil used his own, moistening a cloth pad and wiping his face, trickling a few drops into his mouth. Keith stirred, moaned a little. He sat up, and the mad light was gone from his eyes.

Alison brought her canteen and gave it to him. She looked defiantly at Gil, as if daring him to object.

'It's my water — and he's my brother.'

Gil shrugged and let Keith drink, but not too much. He took the canteen away from him after three swallows.

'Too much would be bad for him at the moment,' he said, handing the bottle back to Alison. 'You'd better drink yourself. How are you feeling?'

'All right.'

She was obviously more concerned for Keith than herself.

Gil said: 'He'll be all right. Touch of the sun — nothing serious.'

He emptied the last of his water on to the cloth pad and moistened the lips of the horses. Their tongues licked eagerly at the dampness. Gil helped Keith back into the saddle of his pony and stared through the haze to the mountains. The sun was going down; soon it would be cooler.

'Stick it out, Keith. We'll be out of the desert by moonrise, and there'll be water in the hills. Let's get going.'

He mounted the bay and nudged the horse with his knees. Keith and Alison followed on their ponies. After sunset the pace quickened; the horses could smell the grass on the hill and knew they were almost out of the desert. The ground became harder, and they broke into a trot. Ahead, trees flanked the hillside, and a stream trickled down from the mountains.

★ ★ ★

Neil Murdoch hurled the empty whisky bottle into a corner and drained the dregs from his glass. He scowled through the window of his shack on

Paradise's main street as Tex moved towards the door. The red-faced giant was hurrying, maybe with news. Murdoch's face was still sore, and he didn't feel like showing himself; he felt that any news must be bad news.

'Boss, Palmer's left town,' the gunman said. 'Headed across the desert. I only just found out, 'cause the boys have been busy ransacking all the empty shacks. I guess they've been gone some time.'

Murdoch swore. 'If I don't do everything myself — Why wasn't someone watching Palmer?'

'I dunno. Guess you didn't say to watch him, boss.'

Murdoch's night-black eyes glittered in his pale face. He put on his coat, adjusted the gun in its shoulder holster.

'Palmer and the Knoxes must have located the clue. Get the boys and saddle up, we're going after them. And get Riggs.'

Tex went out and passed the word round. Slim and the others gathered at the shack; Jamie was not there.

Murdoch glared at Tex. 'I said to get Riggs here.'

'He ain't in town, boss. A Mex said he pulled out, heading for the hills.'

'I should have put a bullet through that rat! Walking out on me now! Well, we can get along without him.'

Slim said: 'What yuh figgering on doing?'

'We'll follow Palmer across the desert. When we catch them, we'll — '

There was a murmur of apprehension from some of the gunmen.

'It's suicide to try to cross the desert. Palmer won't make it, so why should we stick out our necks?'

'That's right,' Slim drawled. 'Why? It's time you opened yore mouth, Murdoch, and let the boys in on this trip. What's so important about catching Palmer — apart from the girl? We know you've got yore eyes on the skirt.'

The gambler looked into Slim's face and saw there a challenge to his authority. With Jamie gone, one man killed and another wounded, he had to keep the rest of the outfit together. If El Lobo rode the treasure trail, Murdoch would need every gun he could muster. He decided it was time to speak.

'Old man Knox hit on a map giving the location of a treasure hoard, worth maybe a hundred thousand bucks or more. It seems that this treasure is the sacred relics of the Aztec Indians, which they brought north and hid when the Spaniards invaded more than three centuries ago. This treasure hasn't been found — till now, no one knew where to look.'

Murdoch paused, looked round the ring of faces, and smiled. He had their interest, every one of them.

'Seth Knox and his partners set out to find the treasure. They didn't, and they never came back; but Knox left a trail to follow. And we're following up that trail. I missed the clue in El Grande, but by tracking Palmer and the girl, we reached Sagebush and got the next clue — leading here, to Paradise.

Now it seems that Palmer has beaten us to it — found the clue to the next stage on the journey. And I aim to go after him, across the desert. That's about it, except, without Riggs, there'll be more to share out.'

Slim said slowly: 'It ain't a-going to be easy, riding across the desert. It'll be hot as hell and there ain't no water-holes. Very few men have ever done it.'

Murdoch laughed softly.

'Scared, Slim?' he jeered. 'Why don't you take a run-out powder, same as Jamie Riggs? Two greenhorns from the east — one of them a girl — are crossing the desert right now. But you get cold feet, and I thought you were a tough hombre!'

The lean man touched his guns. 'I'm coming. I was just pointing out it isn't going to be easy, that's all.'

Murdoch scooped up his black, broad-rimmed hat and jammed it on his head.

'Fill your water canteens and grab

your horses. We're on our way. Palmer won't be able to travel fast with a couple of tenderfeet — likely we'll catch them up before they get out of the desert.' He smiled coldly. 'I'd like to stake Palmer out in the sand and leave him there — and the kid, too. The girl — I've other ideas about her!'

Murdoch led his men outside; they saddled up and rode out of Paradise, heading across the desert towards the mountains.

★ ★ ★

Three Mexican horsemen rode the trail. Jamie, peering from the cover of rocks, recognised the flamboyant garb of the scar-faced Velasquez, and showed himself. Velasquez raised a swarthy hand and the riders halted in front of Jamie.

Jamie didn't waste any time. He said:

'I reckon yuh can take me to El Lobo. I want to talk with that hombre, pronto.'

Velasquez smiled, and said something in Spanish to his men. They laughed, but Jamie didn't understand.

'You hear me, Mex?' Jamie said. 'I want to see The Wolf.'

Velasquez touched the brim of his sombrero and showed white teeth.

'*Si*, Señor Riggs, I hear you very well. You have your horse? Good, we weel ride together. It ees a strange coincidence, but El Lobo, he wants to see you.'

Jamie went back of the rocks and unstaked his gelding; he swung into the saddle and joined Velasquez on the trail. The Mexican said softly:

'You quarrel with Señor Murdoch? Your face, it ees hurt.'

Jamie scowled, touching his bruised face tenderly.

'I'll get Murdoch for this,' he said harshly. 'I aim to fill that hombre plumb full o' lead when I catch up with him.'

They moved off, down the trail, Jamie riding with Velasquez, the two

Mexicans following behind.

'You want to talk about the gold which Señor Murdoch seeks?' Velasquez asked.

Jamie shook his head.

'El Lobo, he trusts Velasquez,' the Mexican hinted.

'More fool him,' Jamie grunted. 'I'm talking to The Wolf, and no one else.'

Velasquez's eyes glinted, and his right hand touched the inlaid butt of his revolver. He suppressed his feelings.

'*Si*, señor, it shall be arranged.'

They rode north of Paradise, skirting the desert, and reached a shack with smoke curling from the chimney. Two Mexicans waited by their horses. They first reported to Velasquez.

'Palmer and the other two started across the desert.'

The second man said: 'Murdoch and his gang are following them.'

Velasquez smiled, and paid for the information. He turned to Jamie, and said:

'You see, Señor Riggs, El Lobo ees

well-informed. He has spies every-where. Now, fill your water bottle, for we, too, must cross the desert. But Velasquez knows a shorter way, where the sand ees hard-packed and the horses can gallop. You are lucky to be with Velasquez, for the trip weel be easier.'

They started out across the desert, travelling fast. Jamie noticed the track had been well-used, and Velasquez commented:

'Only El Lobo's men know this trail. It ees even possible to drive cattle this way.'

They rode hard for hours, not stopping to rest. Velasquez used a quirt on his mount, forcing the pace.

'It ees not good to stop in the desert,' he said between his teeth. 'We weel ride hard and rest when we reach the mountains. To rest here ees dangerous.'

Jamie swigged water from his can-teen, mopped his face and cursed the heat. He flogged his horse to keep up with the Mexican, staring blindly into the shimmering heat haze, knowing he dare not lose his guide. If Velasquez left him, he would surely die.

At last, the sandy waste gave way to cactus and scrub and rock. Clumps of mesquite grass appeared and trees showed in the distance; the sloping hillsides were green and inviting to thirsty men. Velasquez led the way between towering rock walls, to a shack hidden by dense foliage. Mexicans appeared, surrounding them.

Velasquez took Jamie into the hut, where a solitary white man sat at a table. El Lobo rose, spoke in Spanish to his lieutenant, then turned to look at Jamie. He looked a long time and did not seem impressed with what he saw.

Jamie growled: 'For Pete's sake, give me a drink!'

'First,' said The Wolf, 'you will tell me about the gold.'

Jamie watched El Lobo pour a glass of brandy and sip it, enjoying the rich bouquet. Jamie licked parched lips.

'A drink,' he said. 'I can — '

'Afterwards — perhaps.' The Wolf's voice was like the lash of a whip. 'You will talk first, Riggs.'

There was a cold hauteur about El Lobo, a frigid, uncompromising attitude; he was the leader of men and he knew his power. His powerful character impressed itself on Jamie — and the cleft-chinned gunman talked.

He told The Wolf about finding Harper's papers, trailing the Knoxes to El Grande; his meeting with Neil Murdoch, the showdown in Smoky Joe's, where Gil Palmer had taken a hand in the game. El Lobo listened, his eyes fixed on Jamie's face, unspeaking. Jamie's tongue ran on, telling of the journey to Sagebush, the fight in the cemetery, how they had reached Paradise and had been unable to find the next clue. He hinted at the fabulous wealth of the Indian treasure, lost for three centuries.

El Lobo pushed the brandy flask across the table. Jamie grabbed it and drank greedily.

'I shall go after this gold,' El Lobo said. 'It is mine now. I am king in the mountains and everything here belongs to me. Remember that, Riggs. If I allow you a cut of the profits, it is because I am a generous man — you have no rights in the matter.' He smiled a little. 'We shall take care of Murdoch, then see about this man Palmer. Describe him to me.'

'He's a tall, big-boned hombre with clear blue eyes, lantern-jawed. He dresses like any cowpuncher and packs two Colts — and he's the fastest hombre I've seen draw a gun.'

'And he's joined the greenhorns?' El Lobo brooded. 'He sounds an interesting man to meet — I rather pride myself on being fast with a gun. The Knoxes, what of them?'

'Tenderfeet!' Jamie sneered. 'They won't be any trouble.'

'But they're riding the trail. Maybe they know more about this treasure than you do, Riggs. Maybe they can be persuaded to talk.' El Lobo rose to his feet and gave orders in Spanish to the Mexicans. Velasquez went out of the hut and The Wolf turned again to Jamie. 'My reports say that one of the Knoxes looks like a woman dressed as a man. Do you know anything about that?'

Jamie wanted to lie. He didn't trust women and didn't want El Lobo putting her before the gold, but there was something about The Wolf's eyes that warned him against such a course.

'Yeah,' he grunted. 'One's a girl; brother and sister. Murdoch fancies her — '

El Lobo smiled. 'A white woman? It will be a pleasure to meet her — and now, we ride!'

★   ★   ★

The stream was pellucid, bubbling gently over brightly coloured pebbles as it flowed down from the mountains. Luxurious foliage overhung the banks, and leafy trees, verdant green, swayed in a soft breeze. To Gil Palmer, it was a view of paradise after the terrible journey across the desert. He slipped from the saddle of his bay and turned the horse loose, to drink and graze.

'Don't drink too much yet,' he advised Keith and Alison. 'Take it easy on the water or you'll regret it. Me, I'm going to bathe.'

He stripped off his hot, dusty clothes and plunged into the cool water, floundering happily, rinsing out his dry mouth and drinking a little. Keith followed him in. Alison went a little way upstream, beyond dense shrubbery, where she, too, undressed and bathed in the stream. Moonlight made silver reflections on the water, glinted on mountain peaks towering overhead.

After they had dressed, Alison prepared a cold supper.

'No fire,' Gil said. 'This is El Lobo's territory, and I don't figure to invite him to our camp.'

They ate and bedded down for the night. Gil staked the horses, then found himself a perch on a rocky ledge where he could keep watch. He slept lightly, his Winchester at his side, but no incidents occurred and when he woke the sun was climbing above the horizon.

After breakfast they set off. Gil kept a sharp lookout behind them in case Murdoch should have crossed the desert; ahead for El Lobo's men. But the hills were empty, except for the birds and animals, and they rode all morning without sighting a human being. Gil noticed tracks where men had been, but he kept quiet, not wishing to alarm his companions.

Alison was excited: 'It's beautiful, Gil. Like some wild, untamed country where no man has set foot. Everything is so prolific, the trees, birds, the scents and colours. It was worth coming west, just to see this — and those mountain peaks, white-capped and soaring, like majestic sentinels guarding it all. I don't think I've ever been so happy — this is the real treasure, not a hoard of gold that men fight and kill for.'

They reached the foot of the mountains and stared up at a sheer rock wall that seemed to lean outwards, threatening to fall and bury them. Gil turned west, following the cliff face, letting his horse pick its way over loose stones. Below them, the green belt stretched to the edge of the desert, a splash of brightest emerald. The sound of a waterfall grew louder, began to make speech impossible; it became a deafening roar and the spray drifted across the trail, soaking them.

The fall came down between two immense rock formations, a drop of a hundred feet, churning a white froth in the pool at the bottom. From the pool a river stretched out, winding away between the hills, its swift current carrying deadwood and mountain debris. Gil turned downstream till the river narrowed at a place where willows overhung the banks, almost joining in the middle to form a flimsy bridge.

He nosed his bay into the water, clinging to the branches to prevent his being swept away by the strong current; the bay swam across, clambered up the far bank. Gil unwound his lariat and made a cast; across the river, Alison caught it.

'Make the end fast to yore saddle-horn and hold tight!' he shouted.

The girl obeyed and headed her pony into the stream. The pony came ashore, snorting and shaking itself. Alison's face glowed.

'That was wonderful!' she exclaimed.

Gil laughed, and coiled his lariat to throw again. 'I wonder if yore brother will think so,' he said drily.

He tossed the rope back across the water and Keith Knox fastened his end to the saddle-horn of his pony.

'Hang on!' Gil shouted, and started the bay pulling.

Keith went into the water with every appearance of reluctance, clinging desperately to his pony's back. He came out of the river, shivering and pale; his teeth chattered.

Gil grinned and moved off. The rock

wall was less precipitous this side of the river and the trail had been used recently. Gil kept his eyes open, watching for a way up the mountain range. The afternoon sunlight gleamed on the rocks, showing rich reds and earthy browns, metallic blue-greys, dotted here and there with green shubbery.

Abruptly, round a bed, the cliffs parted to reveal a widening canyon. One side was sheer rock, the other sloped at an easy gradient and a narrow path wound upwards. Gil stopped and looked about him. Here, if Seth Knox had gone up the mountainside, should be the next marker on the trail. His keen eyes searched the valley, moving steadily from wall to wall, scanning niches and crannies. He grunted, seeing what he had looked for, and rode towards it.

The rock cairn was overgrown with weeds and, unless a man was looking for it, could have been passed without notice. Gil dismounted and kicked at the pile of rocks with his boot. He dislodged the surface stones, then started digging with his hands. Underneath, his groping fingers felt something smooth. He pulled out a package wrapped in oilskin and undid it.

Alison and Keith crowded at his shoulder as he smoothed out the parchment to reveal the message, scrawled in faded ink:

'Eagle Rock at the top of
the mountain path.'

Gil stared up the cliff-face, thinking it wasn't going to be as easy as it looked. Sure, the first hundred feet or so was easy enough, a smooth gradient, but after that, the climb steepened, the path narrowed — and the drop would be instant death if a horse missed its footing.

'I reckon — ' he started, and broke off as the sound of galloping hoofs sounded down the canyon. He turned, saw Murdoch's outfit approaching at speed. Guns echoed and shells furrowed the earth about him. He wheeled his bay, grim-faced.

'There's only one way now — up the mountain!'

He used his spurs and the bay raced across the open, heading for the narrow rock path winding up into the mountains.

5

Gil took the lead up the rocky path, his eyes alert for a place where they could make their stand. It would be useless trying to outrun Murdoch's outfit in such a terrain. Alison and Keith were close behind, crouched low over their ponies to dodge the flying lead.

Murdoch rode at the head of his men, Colt blazing. The other gunmen crowded him, loosing off shells at the fleeing trio. It was lucky for Gil's party that conditions made accurate shooting difficult. With a sheer drop on one side of the path, the outlaws were too intent on keeping their horses close to the rock wall to bother with aiming their guns. But Gil knew he daren't rely on luck much longer; sooner or later, a flying bullet was going to strike home.

The bay was snorting under the climb, shying at the terrifying drop so close at its heels. Round a bend, the path rose sharply, narrowing dangerously; there was a depression in the cliff-face, opening into a narrow gully. Gil really had no choice about it; with Murdoch so close behind, he had to seek cover in a hurry.

He rode into the gully sliding from the saddle, Winchester in hand.

'Alison, get the horses down behind those boulders. Keith, fire at anyone coming up the path!'

He ran back to the entrance of the gully and dropped flat behind the cover of a rock. He poked the barrel of his Winchester over the rock and sighted the path where it came round the cliff-face. Hoofs sounded, pebbles clattered on the path; horses snorted and voices echoed harshly.

The first of Murdoch's men came into view — red-faced Tex. Gil remembered how the man had drygulched him and all the mercy went out of him. He was fighting, not just for his own life — but Alison's. He squeezed the trigger and pumped lead into Tex's mount. The horse went over the brink, throwing its rider into space. Tex screamed as he went down, falling over and over.

Murdoch's voice shouted: 'They've holed up! Dismount and burn 'em out!'

Gil waited, his lantern jaw resting on the stock of his rifle, face tense, blue eyes cold. The palms of his hands sweated. A face showed; Gil fired and the man dodged back. There was a moment's respite and Gil took stock of their position.

Temporarily, they were safe. Murdoch couldn't come up the path, with Gil covering it. The cliff wall protected them from stray shots — but Murdoch controlled the path. Murdoch couldn't get into the gully — but Gil couldn't get out. There was no other exit. The walls were sheer, rising to razor peaks. The horses were under cover, and Keith, white-faced and trembling, crouched with them. Alison joined Gil, a gun in her hand.

One of their attackers tried to climb the rock, seeking a vantage point to snipe at the three holed out in the gully. His boots scraped loose pebbles, warning Gil of the attempt. Gil bobbed up, slammed three shells in quick succession at the climber; the man cursed and released his hold as rock splinters and shells sprayed about his head. He slid hurriedly downwards to the path and jumped for cover.

Alison, at Gil's elbow, asked: 'What are you going to do? I can't see how we're going to get out of here.'

'Wait till dark,' he replied. 'I'll force Murdoch back far enough to let you up the path; then you and yore brother start for Eagle Rock. I'll stay behind and keep Murdoch busy. They won't pass me while I've ammunition left.'

She said: 'I won't leave you, Gil. We'll stay and fight it out together.'

'I can travel fast, once you and Keith are up top. It's the only way.'

The crown of a stetson appeared round the corner, and Gil shot it off the supporting stick. There was no head inside it.

Murdoch's voice came: 'You can't get out, Palmer. We've got you bottled in that gully. You might as well give in — pass over the message and the girl, and I'll let you go free.'

Gil didn't bother to reply. He crawled to a new position and squinted along the barrel of his rifle, waiting for a head to show. He drew a Colt and lay it to hand in case they should try to rush him. Minutes passed, then fresh gunshots echoed.

Gil started up in surprise. The shots had come from lower down the path, behind Murdoch's outfit. Oaths rang out. Murdoch snarled:

'El Lobo! He's cut off our rear!'

Gil ran forward, crouching low. He reached the path and saw Murdoch's men milling in hopeless confusion. In the canyon below, The Wolf's Mexicans were scattered, firing up at the men on the mountain slope. Gil smiled. To be saved by El Lobo was an ironical twist of fate. He added his rifle to the melee.

Murdoch was in a jam now. With Gil above him, shooting down, and El Lobo below, he had to think fast.

'Back down the path,' he shouted above the roar of gunfire. 'Get to the canyon and shoot up those greasers. We can't stay here like rats in a trap!'

He flung himself into the saddle of his horse and rode recklessly down the rock path, his gun blazing out lead at the men below. Gil watched the others follow, holding his fire.

In the canyon El Lobo's men scattered under the sudden attack. Murdoch broke through their ranks; the walls of the canyon echoed and re-echoed with thunderous noise; crimson flame streaked the grey and green landscape.

'We can escape now,' Alison said. 'Let's get to Eagle Rock before they remember we're up here.'

'I reckon not,' Gil drawled. 'Here, we've got a nice little hideout — no one ain't going to shift us without a lot of trouble. Farther up, we don't know what it's like, and El Lobo is at home in these mountains. Nope, I reckon we'll stay right here till we know the result of that fracas down there.'

He started rolling boulders towards the cliff edge, heaping them up till he formed a shoulder-high barricade across the path. He rested his rifle on the rocks and waited.

'No one's coming up while I'm here,' he said easily. 'When it's dark, you and Keith can head for Eagle Rock. No sense in tipping off our next move with all those hombres around.'

He stared down into the valley, recognising Velasquez — and Jamie Riggs. Jamie seemed to have changed sides, for he was fighting with El Lobo against Murdoch. Murdoch, too, recognised his former partner. He wheeled his horse and galloped down on the man who had turned against him.

Jamie had smoking Colts in his hands, but the sight of Murdoch thundering towards him shook his nerve. His first shot went wide, then he was stumbling back, out of the way of the horse, cursing. Murdoch rode like a crazy man, ignoring the lead flying about his head. He wanted revenge.

'Here's where you get yours, you double-crossing rat!' he shouted.

As he rode past, he thrust the muzzle of his gun full into Jamie's face and pulled the trigger.

Murdoch's horse galloped over Jamie's dead body, and he was away. His men, exchanging shots with the Mexican bandits, hared after him, breaking for freedom. A loose shot took the last rider's mount through the rump. The horse squealed in sudden pain and reared. The gunman flew out of the saddle and crashed headfirst into a jagged outcrop of rock.

Gil watched, grimly silent. Murdoch had only Slim and four men left of the outfit which had ridden out of El Grande. Outnumbered, they rode hard down the canyon, not looking back. They soon passed out of sight, and Gil transferred his attention to The Wolf's gang.

A rough count revealed a dozen swarthy-faced Mexicans, but he could hear others below the cliff wall, out of sight. A formidable outfit. He wondered what El Lobo would do — and was not left long in doubt. The bandits grouped and dismounted, lounging at ease, smoking and reloading their guns; two riders started up the mountain path — Velasquez and The Wolf.

Gil waited, tensed. His Winchester covered the path, ready for action.

'Keep down,' he warned the girl at his side. 'And not a word about Eagle Rock.'

Horses' hooves echoed on the rocky slope. Gil leaned on the barricade, his finger taut about the trigger. He judged when the first rider was about to round the bend into sight, and called:

'Hold it! I've got yuh covered!'

A horse and rider appeared, and El Lobo moved into the sights of Gil's Winchester. This was the man he had ridden to get — 'dead or alive', his chief had said — and he shook with a nervous tension, knowing he could not shoot down the bandit in cold blood.

El Lobo sat, stiff as a ramrod, in the saddle of a fine Palomino mare, a beautiful horse as proud as its rider. He was a big man, this renegade who led the Mexicans, immaculately dressed in grey cord breeches tucked into the top of decorated riding-boots; his shirt was white silk, spotless, and he wore a ten-gallon stetson hat. A single Colt .44 was holstered at his waist.

The Wolf's face was tanned, his eyes deep-set above an aquiline nose, his lips full and firm; a pointed spade beard jutted from his chin. Gil regarded his adversary with increased respect; here was no tinhorn gunman, but a born leader.

Gil knew instantly that this proud man would scorn to shoot from ambush. When he killed, it would be face to face, in a fair fight. That he had ridden alone to look down the barrel of

Gil's rifle spoke of a fearless courage. Gil wondered what tragedy had driven such a man outside the law, to associate with Mexican bandits.

'A strange way to greet the man who drove off your enemies,' El Lobo said.

Gil snapped: 'Tell that Mex to come round the bend, where I can see him.'

The Wolf's hands were slack on the reins. He called without turning his head: 'Velasquez.'

The scar-faced Mexican rode into view, a sinister figure despite his gaudy clothes; his missing ear gave him a menacing air, and his glittering eyes and cruel smile had something snake-like about them.

Alison stood up, covering Velasquez with her gun. She had discarded the bandanna and her red hair flowed down in waves over her shoulders.

'Don't move!' she said coolly.

El Lobo removed his stetson with a flourish, making a formal bow.

'Delighted to make your acquaintance, Miss Knox. This is a pleasure I

160

have been promising myself ever since I heard you were in my territory.'

Gil drawled: 'Now you've had the pleasure, turn yore horse and get the hell out of here, and take yore Mex killers with yuh! Pronto!'

El Lobo's eyes moved past Gil to Keith, crouching beside the horses.

'Your brother seems a little shy, Miss Knox. Won't you introduce us?'

Gil said: 'I'll introduce yuh to a Winchester slug if yuh don't hit the trail! I'm getting tired of holding this rifle.'

'Then put it down. You see, Palmer, neither I nor my man, Velasquez, has attempted to use force. I suggest we talk this over in a friendly way. I've rid you of Murdoch's attentions, now let us discuss the matter of the Aztec gold — '

'I reckon,' said Gil bitterly, 'this treasure is just about the worst kept secret of all time.'

The Wolf shrugged. 'I am king here. Any gold hidden in the mountains

161

belongs to me. Do you think that, even if you should find the treasure, I would let you take it out of my territory? I suggest you tell me all you know, and, in return, I will see that you receive a fair share, and an escort back to civilisation.

'Consider the alternative,' El Lobo said, smiling. 'I am determined to take the Aztec treasure for myself. You are three — against great odds — in a country you know nothing about. How long do you think you will last if I turn my men loose on you?'

The Wolf's eyes were fixed on a point behind Gil and Alison, and his voice was raised. Gil realised, stiffening, that he was speaking to Keith; El Lobo had picked out the weakest member of the party and concentrated on him.

'Tell me everything, and I'll guarantee your safety.'

Keith Knox stumbled forward.

'You promise to let us go? I'll tell you. The next clue is — '

Alison whirled up on her brother.

Her hand came up, slapped him across the face.

'Shut up, you — you coward! If you tell him anything, I'll finish with you for good!'

Keith slunk back, his face flushed, muttering under his breath. Alison turned to El Lobo, her chin out, eyes flashing.

'My grandfather discovered the treasure and gave his life in the attempt. I won't hand it over to anyone, so you can take your gunmen and get out! We don't make deals with murderers!'

The Wolf laughed softly and turned his horse. Velasquez started down the mountain path.

'I admire your spirit, Miss Knox,' El Lobo called back, 'but I think you will regret your impulsiveness. I never give up when I am after something. We shall meet again. Adios.'

Gil snapped: 'Next time, El Lobo, come with yore guns in yore hands. I'll be shooting to kill when I set eyes on yuh again.'

The Wolf stared into Gil's blue eyes.

'Next time, Palmer,' he said quietly, 'I'll call you. I'm considered to be pretty fast with a gun myself.'

He flicked the mare's rein and cantered easily down the path, after Velasquez. Gil watched the two bandits join the Mexicans in the canyon below, then the bandits moved off down the canyon, out of sight.

Gil relaxed, wiped clammy sweat from his hands. His throat was dry with the nervousness he always knew when facing a killer, knowing he might have to kill for his own life. His orders were 'dead or alive', and El Lobo was not the man to let himself be taken alive. Sooner or later, they would come face to face for a second time, and guns would roar sudden death. Gil was not afraid, but neither was he looking forward to that meeting.

Alison looked at him questioningly.

'Are we going up to Eagle Rock?' she asked.

'As far as we can get before dark.'

Gil led his bay, walking on foot, for the evening twilight was closing in, wreathing the mountains in a grey, uncertain light. He was worried in case El Lobo should know another way up the mountain. If the Mexicans got to the top first, Gil's party would be trapped. In mountain warfare, it was the man shooting down who had the advantage.

They went up carefully, hugging the rock wall, their eyes avoiding the drop on the other side of the path. The ponies shied a little, snorting their fear at the hazardous journey into the mountains. Up and up, climbing steadily, the light fading as a dull red sun sank below the horizon. It grew colder and a damp mist hung in the air, seeping through their clothes. Higher up, a dark cave opened into the mountainside, and Gil stopped.

'We'll stay here. No fire, I'm afraid. I'll keep watch while you prepare supper. Afterwards, you can sleep — it would be foolish to continue this climb in the dark. Eagle Rock can wait till tomorrow.'

Later, while Gil was eating the cold supper she had made, Alison asked:

'Do you think The Wolf will bother us again?'

'Not yet. Not till we've unearthed the treasure.' Gil brooded on it. 'El Lobo's a mighty smart hombre; he won't rush in and spoil his chances. He'll wait till we've found the gold for him, then he'll strike.'

Alison said: 'And Murdoch?'

Gil had finished eating. He didn't want to risk lighting a cigarette and giving their position away, so he cut a hunk of tobacco and chewed on it.

'Murdoch's keen on getting his hands on the treasure, but whether he's got the guts to stand against The Wolf I don't know. Maybe. Money is a strange thing; it can make the biggest coward face the greatest odds — sometimes.'

He walked to the mouth of the cave and squatted on a blanket, Winchester across his knees.

'Get some sleep now. You won't be bothered in the night.'

★   ★   ★

It rained a little, then the clouds parted and a silver moon shone through, making ghostly patterns on distant mountain peaks. Gil's eyes searched the cave, saw the blanketed figures of Keith and Alison, still and sleeping. A coyote's howl broke the stillness, but neither of the sleepers stirred; they were worn out by the hazardous climb.

Gil sat staring across the emptiness beyond the edge of the path, trying to plan a course of action. His job was to get El Lobo; that was why he had been sent to the border country. And here he sat, like a watchdog, looking after a couple of greenhorns.

The Wolf could not be far away, and all the time he was free he represented a menace to Alison. It seemed, to Gil, that he could best serve the girl by going after El Lobo and forcing a showdown. If he waited for The Wolf to show up it would be when it suited the bandit.

Gil sighed, and shifted the weight of his rifle. He didn't like the idea of leaving Alison; her brother would be no protection if trouble came while he was absent. But the more Gil thought about it the surer he became that his best move was to track down El Lobo and kill him. Now that he had met the renegade face to face he knew there could be no possibility of taking him alive.

Gil didn't know where El Lobo had his hideout, but one thing would bring him running — the Aztec treasure. If Gil could locate the gold and use it as bait — But he'd have to keep Alison out of it. Suppose the clue at Eagle Rock gave the position of the treasure? The idea developed in his head. He would go to Eagle Rock, follow up the treasure trail alone, and bait a trap for The Wolf.

The horses were sleeping at the back of the cave. Quietly Gil prepared to leave. He wrote a message for Alison and weighted it with a stone, checked his guns and provisions, and roused the bay. The horse was well trained; it moved without waking the ponies. Gil led the bay out of the cave on to the ledge. He gazed back — Alison slept soundly, her red hair draped across one shoulder, outside the blanket.

'I'll be back,' he promised silently.

He led the bay by the reins, walking up the path. The path was narrower, the drop greater; loose stones scuffled underfoot, plunged over the brink. The light of the moon was a flickering thing as cloud-banks overcast the sky; the bay began to whinny. Gil quietened the horse by stroking its muzzle and speaking softly. They went on and up.

A chill breeze soughed about the mountains, and in the distance Gil caught his first glimpse of Eagle Rock. Through the mist it appeared like a great bird, wings outspread in flight, a massive chunk of rock weathered to the shape of an eagle. Gil continued the climb, heading towards Eagle Rock.

The narrow ledge was treacherous, the edge crumbling. Gil sweated, clinging to the rock face rising sheer, bulging out over his head; he kept the reins of the bay taut, leading the horse behind him. It became steeper, and Gil had to release his mount, to let it make its own way after him. He scrambled forwards on hands and knees, cursing the wavering moonlight. Stones slithered past him, starting a miniature avalanche; he pressed himself flat against the rock, hands wrapped about a jutting crag, the wind whistling about him.

The clouds passed, and silver moonbeams lanced down, revealing the awful drop inches away. His eye caught sight of something below, and he stared at it, not realising for long moments that he was looking at the skeleton of a man who had once slipped over the edge. The bones were twisted into an appalling position.

Gil lay still, breathing heavily. An idea

formed in his head. Suppose these were the bones of Seth Knox? Suppose the old man had never reached Eagle Rock? Any clue there was lay down below, with those bleached and broken bones.

Gil studied the drop carefully. The dead man had not plummeted to the bottom of the mountain; he lay across a jutting ledge, wedged to the cliff by the stump of a tree that grew there. A little mesquite grass sprouted from the earth in the niche; mosses made a green carpet between the disjointed bones of the skeleton. Gil calculated that his lariat was too short to reach the ledge; but the rock wall below was rough enough to give him hand and footholds. He decided to go down.

He made the bay lie down on the path and unhooked his lariat. An outcrop of rock served at a hitching-post; he made fast the rope and threw the end over the cliff-edge. It uncoiled, swinging some feet above the ledge where the skeleton lay. He tested the rope. It held, and he swung himself into space, lowering himself hand over hand, gripping the rawhide tightly in his sweaty hands.

He went down slowly, cautiously, searching for footholds to take some of the strain off his arms. The rope swung a little. Anxiously he watched the end, trying to keep his eyes off the terrible drop below the ledge. He heard a noise; the bay was whinnying. Something — or someone — had disturbed it. Gil looked up.

A swarthy face peered over the edge, grinning down at him. A naked steel blade flashed in the moonlight, sliced through the rope. Gil felt himself falling; air rushed past him, then something hit him with stunning force and he blacked out.

★ ★ ★

Keith Knox woke suddenly, wondering what had disturbed him. He half rose in his blankets, leaning on one elbow and staring about him. The cave was quiet;

Alison was still sleeping. Moonlight shafted in through the mouth of the cave, gleamed on distant mountain peaks. The ponies huddled together in the darkest corner of the tiny cave.

Then he realised what it was that had been bothering him. Gil was no longer squatting at the cave mouth. Keith glanced back; the bay had gone, too. He rolled out of his blankets and searched carefully. There was no sign that Gil had ever been there. His horse, blankets, rifle, all were gone. Keith went on to the ledge and looked up and down the mountain path — and saw nothing. The night air was still.

So he's deserted us, Keith thought, and smiled. Now, perhaps, Alison would consider returning, giving up this insane quest. His eye caught a paper on the ground, weighted with a stone. He picked up the message and read:

'Dear Alison — I have gone after El Lobo. Sit tight till I return. You will be safe enough in the cave for the time being. I don't think I shall be long.

'Your friend,
GIL PALMER.'

Keith crumpled the paper in his hand, stood frowning. Suppose Alison never saw this message? The idea grew — if she believed Gil had left her! Keith wanted only one thing, to get out of the mountains, back east to the comfort and safety he had always known. He made up his mind, glanced again at the sleeping girl, then strode to the edge of the cliff and tossed the paper over. A gust of wind caught the paper, swept it down the canyon till it was out of sight.

He went back to the cave and woke his sister.

'Palmer's gone,' he said. 'Deserted. Run out on us.'

Alison stirred. His words hit her like icy water, and she came out of her blankets in a hurry. Sleep dropped away from her eyes as she saw that Gil and the bay were no longer in the cave. A coldness clutched at her heart; she fought for calmness.

'Don't be silly, Keith. Gil can't be far away. He probably heard a noise and went to investigate.'

'Taking his horse? And blankets?'

Alison clutched her gun and went on to the path, staring into the moonlit emptiness. She raised her voice, called:

'Gil — Gil!'

Only the whispering of the wind answered her. She fought her doubts.

'Go back to sleep, Keith. I'll keep watch till Gil returns.'

'He won't come back, sis. You were a fool to trust him. Let's go back east. Even you can't mean to go on now. These terrible mountains — and El Lobo — and Murdoch. Alison, we must turn back. Can't you see that?'

Alison was disturbed by Gil's absence. Surely he would have woken her, or left a message? Had anything happened to him?

'Gil will return,' she said, but her tone lacked confidence.

Keith laughed sourly. 'What a hope!'

Alison turned as a sound on the path outside the cave attracted her attention. Someone had dislodged a stone; it rattled among the rocks before it fell silently into space. Alison sighed with relief and turned towards the cave mouth.

'Gil! I'm so glad — '

The words died in her throat. There was no answer. She gripped her revolver tightly.

'Gil! Is that you?'

Keith stirred uneasily, backing behind his sister. He began to wish that Gil would come back. Alison called again:

'Who's there? I've got you covered.'

She pointed the muzzle of her gun at the mouth of the cave, her finger taut on the trigger. If it was one of El Lobo's men — Her pulses quickened and she prayed Gil would hurry back. A dark cloud moved across the sky, blotting out the moonlight. She could see nothing; then two green eyes glittered in the darkness. Alison froze, a scream choking in her throat.

The cloud passed and she saw, framed in the mouth of the cave, the sleek, tawny body of a mountain lion. Its coat was shiny with a damp mist, its cruel eyes stared at her. The big cat crouched, whiskers bristling, lips curled. It roared once, prepared to spring.

Alison, white-faced, jerked the trigger three times as the lion hurled forward. Three slugs smashed into its head, then the huge body knocked her backwards. She grabbed at the rock wall, turned her gun to fire again, but the savage animal lay still on the ground. Her shots had penetrated the brain, killing it instantly.

The big cat sprawled like a fantastic carpet over the bare rock, blood seeping from its head, eyes glazed and lifeless. Alison panted for breath, leaning against the wall. The ponies were awake, tramping the ground, whinnying in fear at the cat smell. Keith huddled limply in a corner, trembling.

Alison pulled herself together. She quietened the ponies, then went out to the rocky path, searching carefully; it occurred to her that the lion might have a mate close by, and she had her gun ready. But the path was deserted, the mountain silent under a ghostly light. She returned to the cave and, with Keith's help, dragged the body of the dead lion to the edge of the cliff and pitched it over.

She moved her blankets to the cave entrance and reloaded the empty chambers of her revolver, settling down to keep guard. Keith joined her, feeling restless, unable to sleep. Now that he had got over the shock of the lion's attack, he was eager to persuade his sister to return east.

He said: 'If Gil intended coming back, he'd be here by now. Those shots would sound for miles in the mountains. He must have heard them.'

Which was exactly what Alison had been thinking. Surely Keith could not be right? Had Gil left her?

'He'll be on his way back now,' she said, without conviction.

A half-hour passed, and Gil did not return. Alison stirred restlessly; she remembered once before when Gil had been away all night, how bitterly she had regretted her doubts then. He'd fought off Murdoch's gang, stood between her and El Lobo; surely he would not desert her now?

The night hours dragged on, hours of tortured doubt for Alison. If only Gil hadn't taken his horse and blankets, left something to prove he intended to return!

Keith said: 'You little fool, Alison. I believe you've fallen in love with Palmer! He's no good — you're better off without him. Now, when we get home — '

'Oh, shut up!'

Keith was silent again, a little scared of his sister's brooding quietness. He had never seen her like this before. The red flush of dawn stippled the mountain peaks, crept through the valleys and canyons. Keith prepared a cold breakfast, leaving his sister alone with her thoughts.

Why doesn't he come back? Why? Tears, frozen and salty, clung to the corners of her eyes, stained her cheeks. Her hands hugged the steel barrel of the gun till her fingers were numbed and forgotten. All was forgotten — all, except the terrible fear that the man she loved might not return.

Keith said awkwardly: 'Breakfast, Alison. You must try to eat something.' He added: 'It won't be so bad, going down the mountain.'

She said nothing, pecked at the food he brought her, without appetite. Keith packed the blankets and saddled both ponies, leading them to the mouth of the cave.

'Come on, sis,' he urged. 'Let's get down to the bottom, out of this horrible place.'

Her voice was hollow, unrecognisable.

'I'm staying till Gil shows up.'

He hesitated, scowled, and sat down to wait. A half-hour passed. The sun climbed higher, but Gil Palmer did not return.

Keith said: 'It's no use staying here. Palmer's gone for good. I'm going down, you follow when you're ready. I'll wait for you at the bottom.'

His words had no effect on her. He led his pony on to the narrow mountain track and started down, confident that she would follow in a little while — there was nothing else she could do.

Alone, Alison's thoughts turned to her grandfather's treasure, which had brought her to the West. She had little interest in it now, but she hadn't come all that way just to give up at the last stretch. She would go on to Eagle Rock. Gil had deserted her, Keith turned back, but she would go on in spite of everything. She took the reins of her Indian pony and began to climb the narrow path towards Eagle Rock.

6

Murdoch did not ride far. As soon as it became obvious that El Lobo's Mexicans were not following, he reined in his horse and stopped. Slim and the others checked their mounts and waited, taking the opportunity to reload their guns. Their horses grazed on the grass in the canyon.

Murdoch climbed a rock to study the position. He seethed with anger at being so close to the treasure — and the girl — then to be balked by The Wolf.

From the top of a rock he could look down the canyon. He saw the Mexicans idling in a group, watched El Lobo and Velasquez ride up the mountain path, to return half an hour later. Then the whole outfit moved off, making no attempt to get at the three barricaded on the mountainside.

Murdoch looked puzzled. Why didn't

he use the superior force of his numbers to gain the upper hand? It looked as if El Lobo was withdrawing, leaving Palmer and the Knoxes a clear field. He was thoughtful as he climbed down to rejoin his men.

'I reckon,' Slim drawled, 'from the way you're ambling along, that we ain't in no danger from the Mex outfit.'

Murdoch didn't miss the note of sarcasm in his voice. He stared into the lean brown face of the lanky gunman and saw open rebellion. Slim was going to be a threat to his authority — if he was allowed to live. He said:

'I'm the boss, Slim.'

'Some boss! Your partner double-crosses yuh, and we lost three men — without getting any nearer the treasure, if it exists.'

He half turned, glanced at the other gunmen. 'Me, I'm pulling out afore El Lobo gets on our trail again. You fellers coming with me?'

They glanced at Murdoch, hesitating.

'Waal,' said one casually, avoiding

Murdoch's piercing eyes. 'It seems we ain't a-going to get the gold, not with The Wolf sticking his nose in. That Mex outfit sure outnumbers us plenty. And they're at home in the mountains.'

His cronies grunted assent. 'Yeah, there ain't much point in hanging around now.'

Murdoch's granite face was expressionless. He bit the end off a cheroot and lit up, carelessly releasing the buttons of his coat so that he could get at his shoulder gun quickly. Slim missed his move.

'Listen, you hombres,' the gambler said, puffing at his cheroot, 'there's a fortune in those mountains, and I aim to get it. El Lobo's pulled out, leaving Palmer and the kids a free run. I figure The Wolf intends to let them find the gold, then step in and grab it. Well, I aim to beat him to it. Move in before he's ready, liquidate Palmer, and — '

'And grab the girl!' Slim finished. 'Me, I'm heading back for El Grande, pronto.'

He swung himself up into the saddle of his mount. Murdoch's voice checked him:

'You're not going anywhere, Slim!'

The gunman stiffened, reading the menace in Murdoch's tone. He went for his guns, but Murdoch cleared holster first. His long-barrelled Colt swept from under his coat, spitting lead. Red flame stabbed out, thunder roared across the canyon, the air reeked of cordite. Slim jerked in the saddle, slumping, his gun-arm falling slack. He toppled to the ground and huddled in a lifeless heap, blood staining his shirt.

Murdoch holstered his gun. 'You jaspers can forget about going home yet awhiles!' he said coldly. 'I don't allow anyone to run out on me. We're going after the gold!'

The gunmen moved uncertainly, taken aback at the cold-blooded murder of Slim. The look in Murdoch's night-black eyes warned them that now was no time for getting ideas.

'I reckon,' drawled one, 'that we're

185

heading into the mountains.'

Murdoch laughed. 'Just keep that notion in the forefront of your minds.' He glanced up at the narrow path merging into the rock face with the approach of dusk. 'At dawn. I don't reckon to make that climb in the dark, not with El Lobo's bandits around. We'll make camp and rest up. Tomorrow, we'll show The Wolf he ain't the only hombre along the border with brains!'

He mounted and led his four remaining men along the canyon, stopping at a hollow of rocks, backed by sheer cliff. It was an ideal hide-out and Murdoch promptly made camp. He allowed no fire, and the supper was cold; afterwards he bedded down, leaving the gunmen to divide the night watch between them. He slept restlessly, dreaming of a girl with red hair. Soon she would be in his hands —

A little after dawn, Murdoch and his men rose, watered their horses, ate breakfast, and checked their guns.

Murdoch took the lead down the canyon, moving slowly and with little noise, eyes alert for signs of El Lobo. But the canyon appeared deserted. All was quiet. The narrow path winding up into the mountains was empty, the early morning sun bright on shards of rock.

Round a bend in the canyon they came upon the scene of yesterday's battle; vultures, disturbed at their scavenging, soared into the air, wheeling about, waiting to come down again when the men had passed. Murdoch cursed under his breath; if El Lobo was watching the canyon, the vultures' sudden flight would warn him of their approach. He stood up in his stirrups, scanning the canyon walls; there were a hundred secret places for hidden eyes. The silence was forbidding, threatening.

Rifle fire crackled, echoing harshly between the narrow walls. Murdoch wheeled about, drawing his gun. Two of his men dropped at the first volley, riddled with lead. The air was stabbed with crimson flame and puffs of black smoke. Lead shells furrowed the ground, whined off rock walls.

'Ambushed!' Murdoch shouted. 'Ride for it — we're in a trap!'

The men in the canyon walls were well hidden, impossible to get at. Murdoch and his two riders could only run for their lives, unable to fight back. But El Lobo had planned well; a line of horsemen came down the canyon, firing steadily. The hail of lead swept away horse and rider, and Murdoch and his sole gunman turned and galloped back through the criss-crossing rifle fire from the rock walls. They used spurs and quirts to flog their mounts, crouching low, hardly daring to hope they could run the gauntlet and get clear with their lives.

Murdoch's gunman threw up his hands as a slug tore through his chest; he crashed off his horse into the rocks. The Mexicans behind Murdoch stopped firing and reduced their pace to a canter; those in the rock walls reloaded their rifles and held their fire. Murdoch could hardly believe his good luck; he was going to break through — then he saw the second line of men drawn across the canyon ahead of him. El Lobo's ambush was complete; there was no avenue of escape left him.

Murdoch, snarling, drew his gun and raced on. He'd take some of the greasers with him before they finished him. El Lobo's voice rang out:

'Surrender, Murdoch! You can't escape!' In Spanish, he gave orders to his men: 'Don't shoot — I want him taken alive!'

But the gambler didn't trust El Lobo. He rode on recklessly, threatening to break through their lines. A lariat whirled out, noosed about his horse's hind legs and brought the animal to the ground. Murdoch hit the ground and rolled over, the breath knocked out of him. He lay gasping, unable to move; two Mexicans took his gun away and hauled him upright as El Lobo rode up on his Palomino mare.

The Wolf stroked his beard and looked down at the dust-covered gambler, his face hard and unsmiling. Murdoch snarled an oath.

Mexicans pressed about the gambler, prodding him with guns. Swarthy faces grinned at him, faces that had no mercy in them. El Lobo sat stiffly in the saddle, his white shirt immaculate, his ten-gallon hat square on his head.

'You were a fool to come back, Murdoch,' The Wolf said, 'but I knew you would. A man of your calibre thinks only of gold — and the girl! — so I waited in ambush. Your forces have been eliminated and you are my prisoner. Now, you will tell me all you know about the Aztec treasure!'

A cunning light gleamed in Murdoch's eyes. El Lobo's only knowledge of the gold had come through Jamie Riggs — and Jamie was dead. So The Wolf lacked information; that was why he had taken the gambler alive. Murdoch saw his chance; the chance to force a bargain.

'Maybe we can form a partnership?' he suggested. 'Your men — and my knowledge. Split the gold fifty-fifty and I'll talk. Those are my terms. Take it or leave it.' He added, as an afterthought: 'And I want the girl, Alison.'

El Lobo frowned, his face darkening with anger.

'You fool! Do you think you can bargain with me, Murdoch, when I hold your life in my hands? You'll talk — or I'll turn you over to Velasquez to loosen your tongue!'

Murdoch paled. Velasquez grinned, waving a knife under the gambler's nose.

'*Si*, Señor Wolf, give him to me to play with. Señor Murdoch weel talk pronto if I heat the blade of my knife and apply it to his feet. The feet are so tender!'

Murdoch shuddered, inching away from Velasquez.

'All right, I'll talk, El Lobo. I'll tell you all I know — but you'll give me a

191

cut of the gold? You can't leave me out — '

The Wolf said contemptuously: 'Just talk, Murdoch. Afterwards, I'll decide what is to be done with you — what you're worth. I am king in the mountains — the dispenser of life and death. It is not your place to haggle with me. Talk!'

Murdoch licked his lips, sweating. He was in a tight corner, and he knew it. There didn't seem to be any way out; he had to talk and take a chance on El Lobo sparing his life.

'Here it is,' he started, 'all I know — '

Velasquez hissed: 'Quiet! Señor Wolf, someone comes down the mountain path!'

El Lobo snapped orders in Spanish: 'Take cover. Keep Murdoch quiet — and don't open fire till we see who it is!'

His men melted away, vanishing amongst the rocks. El Lobo, with Velasquez and Murdoch, moved behind an overhang of the cliff face, silent and waiting. The canyon was still, seemingly deserted, and the vultures came down. Footfalls sounded on the narrow path, coming nearer.

★ ★ ★

Consciousness returned with sharp pain, a cold wind whistling about him, a grey pre-dawn light. Gil Palmer tried to remember things — where he was, what had happened. He forced his eyes wide open, shifted his head from side to side.

He was lying in mid-air, or so it seemed at first. Bare rocks extended to his left and right; reared high above him. A terrifying drop emptied away below; he closed his eyes, dizzy, and shook his head to clear it. The sudden movement brought pain and he lay still for some minutes, memory flooding back.

The memory of setting off for Eagle Rock, noticed the skeleton — of Seth Knox? — below on the cliff ledge, climbing down — then the swarthy-faced Mexican and his glittering knife.

The drop through space as he cut the rope. It all came back, fitting into place.

Gil opened his eyes again. He was lying on the same ledge as the skeleton, precariously perched, in imminent danger of completing the fall to the bottom of the mountain. He rolled back from the edge, pressing hard against the rock wall, gritting his teeth as sudden agony swept through his body. It was almost a miracle he had not been killed — a few more inches and he would have missed the ledge, plummeted down to certain death hundreds of feet below. The ledge had saved him — and it was only because he had been more than half-way down when he fell, that he still lived. If he had fallen from the top —

Gil used his hands, feeling the bones in his body gently, relieved to discover that none were broken. He was bruised and scratched and dried blood was clotted on his face; he stretched carefully, ignoring spasms of pain. Glancing up, he saw that his lariat had completely disappeared; he was trapped on the ledge — with a terrifying drop beneath him.

He lay still for a while, resting, considering what to do. Somehow, he had to climb the rock face; that meant waiting till he had more light. He wondered about Alison; had she missed him? And the Mexican who had cut the rope; was he still snooping around on the mountain path?

Gil turned his attention to the skeleton. The bones had been picked clean by the vultures, the clothes rotted away. He dug into the moss and lichen with his fingers, discovered an oilskin package almost buried in the scanty earth. He wiped it dry and clean and unfolded it to find a parchment map — and the signature of Seth Knox.

He knew now that he had found Alison's missing grandfather — and the map giving the position of the Aztec gold. The original writing was almost a picture language, easy to understand. The map showed Eagle Rock and a path leading over the mountains to a cave; it was here the treasure had been buried. Gil studied it closely, memorised the route, then rolled and lit a cigarette; with the quirly drawing well, he held the match to the parchment and set fire to the map. He crumbled the ashes and tossed them into space. Neither El Lobo nor Murdoch would get the treasure now; he would reveal its position only to Alison — and there would be no clue at Eagle Rock.

Dawn arrived, flushing the rocks with red light. Gil spent his time studying the wall above him, noting clefts and crags that he could use when he attempted the climb. It was not going to be easy. If he made one bad guess, used a hold that gave way, he would drop to his death; he could hardly hope to land on the narrow ledge a second time. When he went up, he would have to be very sure of himself, of his strength, of his ability to avoid looking down. The depths below had a dreadful fascination; he practised keeping his eyes turned upwards.

Time passed. He drew a deep breath and started the climb. He reached up, dug his fingers into a cleft in the rock, tested it for security. He was almost afraid to take his feet off the ledge, to place his whole weight on the inch or so of fingerhold he had. He forced himself to pull up one leg, then the other, not daring to look down, but finding toe-grips by scraping the cliffs with his boots digging in, wedging himself. He continued upwards.

Like a fly on a wall, he moved slowly, sweating, his arms and legs beginning to ache under the strain. One hand going up, one foot; then the other hand, the other foot. The strain was tremendous; the wind lashed him whining eerily, reminding him of the drop if he failed. He studied each hold before going on, reaching up, testing it; he trained himself to remember footholds so that he could find them without looking down. He kept a picture of Alison in his mind, telling himself he must not fail for her sake.

The sun rose higher. Gil stopped suddenly, hearing footsteps on the path overhead. He listened carefully, trying to decide who it was. One person, one horse, moving up the mountain track to Eagle Rock. Should he call out? A rope thrown from above would save him — but suppose whoever it was up there was an enemy? The Mexican who had cut the rope? Gil knew he would get no second chance. He could not risk shouting out — and there was only one person on the trail. The sounds were unmistakable.

Alison and Keith would be together — but then, he'd told them to stay in the cave, in his message. He began to sweat, wondering what had happened at the cave. This man must have passed there — the footfalls faded away farther up the mountainside and Gil continued with his climb. He dare not hurry, even though he was worried over Alison; each hold must be tested before he put his full weight on it. Hand over hand, gasping with exertions, he struggled up towards the path.

A barrage of gunfire echoed in the canyon far below, filling him with doubts. Had Murdoch returned to shoot it out with El Lobo? Or were Alison and Keith in trouble? He could not look down, only struggle upwards, cursing the Mexican who had placed him in such a terrible position. The shooting died out after a while, but Gil had other worries on his mind.

Reaching up for a crag of rock jutting above his head, he lost his hold; loose stones crashed past him and his feet swung in space, scrabbling at the rock wall; he hung suspended by one arm, searching for another grip. Sweat poured down his face; his arm, with the whole weight of his body on it, felt as though it were being wrenched from its socket. Desperately, he dug in his toes, tore his fingernails trying for a grip on the bare rock surface. He found a cleft, clung there, panting for air. He tried to ease the strain off his arms, rested a little.

Looking up, the mountain track seemed no nearer — and he was tiring. He forced himself to go on again, testing each hold with even more care. He reached up, pulling his weary body over the vertical face of the cliff, swaying in the wind. Time passed with agonising slowness. Again, there were the noises of men and horses on the path; about a dozen of them. He held his breath, hanging in silence for the cavalcade to pass. These could only be El Lobo's men, on their way to Eagle Rock. Gil Palmer wondered what had happened at the cave — and swore revenge if any harm had come to Alison.

★　★　★

Keith was half-way down the mountain path when he heard firing in the canyon below. He halted, hesitating, looking back to see if Alison were following, but the path behind him was empty. After a while, the shooting stopped, and he went on again.

He travelled on foot, hugging the rocky wall, afraid to mount and ride the narrow path. He led his pony by the reins, his eyes avoiding the awful drop below. When he came to the gully where Gil had fought off Murdoch's gang, he had to stop and shift the barricade of stones from the path. Then he moved down the easier slope, reaching the foot of the mountain, where mesquite grass swept out to carpet the canyon floor. He saw the body of a man lying on the ground, a little way off, and recognised him as one of Murdoch's men.

A low laugh made him turn, and he saw El Lobo, mounted on his great Palomino mare, watching him from behind an overhang of rock. The Wolf snapped a command in Spanish and dark-skinned Mexicans rose to surround Keith. El Lobo rode forward, removed his ten-gallon hat in a mock bow, and said:

'This is a pleasure, Mr Knox. I hope

your sister will be joining us?'

Keith's face was pale. He licked his lips nervously.

'You promised we could go free,' he mumbled, 'if I told you all I know.'

'But that was last night,' El Lobo said drily. 'Neither your sister nor Palmer seemed anxious to take advantage of my generous offer. I am not sure that the offer is still open. See,' he continued, waving a hand towards Velasquez and his prisoner, 'I have Murdoch now.'

'Palmer's gone,' Keith said. 'I left Alison in the cave — she'll be coming down soon. And I know where the next clue is hidden. If I tell you, you'll let us go? You can have the gold — all I want is to go back east. I'm fed up with this awful country.'

Velasquez sneered: 'This is a country for — men!'

'I don't care what you think of me,' Keith said defiantly. 'I want to go home.'

El Lobo smiled. 'The next clue,' he

said softly, 'where is it?'

All attention was focused on Keith and El Lobo. There was a tension in the air. Murdoch saw that his chance had come — with Keith in The Wolf's power, his own usefulness had come to an abrupt end. He knew he must get away before the bandits killed him. He lunged sideways, grabbing the nearest Mexican's gun, leaping for a horse.

Velasquez was first to see him.

'Murdoch!' he shouted, and fired from the hip.

His slug whined past Murdoch's head. The gambler fired back, winging one of the bandits — then El Lobo drew. His right hand moved with eye-baffling speed, swung the .44 from its holster, and triggered once. The shell sped true to Murdoch's brain, smashed him out of the saddle, to the ground. The gambler would worry Alison no more.

Keith felt sick at the killing. He had no pity to waste on the gambler, but to witness his murder was another thing.

He was a little awed by the speed of The Wolf's gun-hand, too.

El Lobo reloaded the empty chamber in his Colt and holstered it. His voice was calm, unmoved by sudden death.

'The clue, Mr Knox. Where is it? You need waste no sympathy on that rat — I should have killed him anyway.'

Keith shivered, and lowered his eyes; he could not face the direct gaze of the proud, bearded man who sat so stiffly in his saddle. There was something cold and deadly about El Lobo, something frightening in his calm assurance.

'Eagle Rock,' he mumbled. 'The next clue is at Eagle Rock. You won't hurt Alison, will you? You'll let her go, too?'

'Miss Knox,' said The Wolf quietly, 'will receive my closest attention, you may be sure of that. I shall make myself personally responsible for her. And now, we will ride for Eagle Rock.'

He snapped commands in Spanish; Velasquez seized the reins of Keith's pony and guided him towards the mountain path. El Lobo moved into the forefront of his men, leading the way up the trail. He was smiling to himself; yes, he would take care of the girl, very good care. And Palmer — The Wolf kept a sharp lookout for him; the youngster seemed to think that Palmer had deserted the girl, but El Lobo was a better judge of character. He knew that Gil would be back . . . if he lived.

With Keith as hostage, he thought he would command the situation. And, once he had the treasure, then would be time to think of the girl. El Lobo was pleased with the way things had turned out as he climbed higher into the mountains, passing the gully and the barricade Keith had demolished, to reach the cave where Keith and Alison had spent the night.

Keith was amazed to find his sister gone. Could she have fallen over the edge? El Lobo saw the dismay in his face and laughed.

'Your sister,' he said, 'has rather more courage than her brother. Undoubtedly she has gone on to Eagle Rock alone

— we shall find her there, waiting for us.'

El Lobo rode on up the path. He had no doubt that he was right about the girl; only one thing bothered him — had Palmer returned? He shrugged; with Keith a prisoner, Palmer would have his hands tied. He stared above him; there, silhouetted against the sky, reared a giant bird with wings outstretched, a bird carved from stone. Eagle Rock.

* * *

The cavalcade passed, the noise of horses and men fading into the distance as they moved higher up the mountain track. Gil, clinging desperately to the rock face, stretched an arm upwards for the next hold; he was numb, the muscles of his arms and legs aching, his fingers bleeding where the skin had torn on sharp crags.

His boots scraped the cliff wall, digging for toeholds. He was panting with his exertions, trying to hurry, knowing he dare not take the slightest risk. Worry gnawed at his mind; had The Wolf captured Alison? Had she been one of the riders who passed on the way to Eagle Rock? If Gil had ever had doubts that he loved Alison Knox, they were resolved in that moment. His whole being was intent upon reaching the path above, tracking down El Lobo and killing him, saving the girl he loved.

The path was no more than twenty feet above his head, but the sheer wall seemed smooth as calmed water, bulging outwards to make his ascent more dangerous.

Gil's twin Colt .45s slapped his thighs as he climbed, the weight of them urging him on; his hands itched with the desire to face El Lobo, to draw his irons and pour hot lead into the renegade who threatened Alison's safety. It was strangely quiet in the mountains; only the sighing wind, his own breath and the scraping of his boots on hard rock broke the heavy silence all around. Wearily, he reached up, feeling the barren smoothness over his head, shifting the weight of his body on cramped legs, searching for another hold. He pulled himself up another six inches, rested, reached up again. The wall seemed to tilt outward at an alarming angle, threatening him with disaster.

He hugged the cliff, feeling the additional strain on his arms; now, his legs swung free, out from the sheer, smooth rock. Desperately he reached up, trying to surmount the bulge of the mountain, to attain the path that loomed so short a distance overhead. His boots scraped rock again, and he knew he had passed the worst. His clawing fingers stubbed at the brink of the path, reached over the edge, held — he heaved himself up, got his shoulder over, wriggled upward. He threw one leg sideways, levering his body — then he was up, rolling on to the flat path that wound along the mountainside. Panting, he lay still, suddenly exhausted by the absence of his need to struggle further. He was safe; he could relax . . .

Gil climbed to his feet. There was only one thought in his mind; El Lobo — and Alison. He had to reach Eagle Rock. Automatically, he checked his guns, then started up the path. His horse was gone; the Mexican would have taken that, of course — and with it his rifle and spare ammunition, his blankets and provisions. He was alone, on foot, with only his .45s to combat the toughest outfit on the border. But Gil did not think of turning back. He thought only of the girl he loved as he plodded wearily towards Eagle Rock. It was a personal matter, now, between Gil Palmer and El Lobo.

He toiled upwards, legs aching, panting for breath. Round a bend in the track, he came upon Eagle Rock. The stone bird spread giant wings over a lonely plateau and Gil, crouching low behind a rock, had a perfect view of the scene.

He saw no one. There was no sound; only tracks in the dust indicated that horsemen had been there — and gone. He saw no sign of Alison. His heart sank. Where was El Lobo's hideout? Where had the renegade taken the girl? He came from cover and approached Eagle Rock. No point in searching for the clue he knew did not exist; the secret of the Aztec treasure was safe in his head. He knew what he must do; locate the hidden gold and use it as bait for The Wolf. Temporarily, he must forget Alison and follow the treasure trail . . . but he was reluctant to leave her.

A startled voice said: 'Señor Palmer! So you still live!'

Gil looked up at Eagle Rock — and Velasquez. Then the Mexican sprang at him, knife in hand.

*　*　*

Alison rode unhurriedly up the mountain track, leaving the pony to find its

210

own way. She was hardly aware of the sheer drop inches away from her. The man she loved had deserted her. The thought went round and round inside her head. She rode as if in a dream, ignoring the glory of sunlight on distant mountain peaks, the magnificent view, the clean, sharp air.

The path narrowed, grew suddenly steeper, more treacherous, and her Indian pony stopped. She dismounted, and climbed on foot, leading the pony by its reins. Higher and higher she climbed till, at last, she sighted Eagle Rock. The huge stone bird meant nothing now; she went on by reflex action, because she could not bear to sit still and think of Gil. She had to do something . . . so she continued on the trail to the next clue her grandfather had left.

All the time she prayed she would see Gil waiting for her on the mountain-path; but the barren rocks remained deserted. Her last hope was shattered when she reached the bleak plateau and saw that Gil was not there. She sat on a rock, her face buried between her hands, crying. Even tears no longer meant anything; she was an aching void, without the desire to live.

After a time she brushed the tears from her eyes and stood up. She began to search the plateau, delving into tiny clefts in the rock, scratching at a heap of stones that might be a cairn marking the place her grandfather had left his message. She found nothing. Eagle Rock was not giving up its secret — if it had one — and she wished Gil was there. He would find it . . .

Her pony was restless, pawing the ground, snorting. Alison wondered if he sensed as someone approached; she called:

'Gil? Is that you, Gil? Is anyone there?'

There was no answer. Only the wind whistled through the rocks. She sat down again, trying to make up her mind what to do. She no longer had any interest in finding the Aztec gold — she might as well return east. But then her last chance of seeing Gil would be gone and, though he had left her, she knew she still loved him and would take him back if he returned.

She remembered Keith. Her brother had gone down the mountain; had said he'd wait for her at the bottom. She must go down to him — he needed her. But she wouldn't leave yet. First, she must resolve her own mind, try to put Gil Palmer out of her thoughts. She needed to be alone to think . . .

The sounds of horses and men drifted up from the mountain-path. Alison started. Could it be Gil? But she heard the voices of men talking in Spanish and knew it was El Lobo who approached. Should she hide? She looked round at the bleak rocks, the winding track between the mountains, and shook her head. It was useless to run. The Wolf would soon find her; better to face him now. She remembered that her brother had gone down the path and became anxious for him.

He must have run into El Lobo's men. She prayed that no harm had come to him.

She stood up, drawing her gun and facing the trail. Eagle Rock towered above her, the shadow of outstretched wings falling across her face like some ominous thunder-cloud. There was a tension in the air, as if a storm approached. Then El Lobo rode into view on his Palomino mare.

The leader of the Mexican bandits swept off his ten-gallon stetson and bowed, smiling at her.

'A pleasure, Miss Knox. I felt sure I should find you here — how glad I am to be proved right.'

Alison kept her revolver levelled at him. She felt calmer now that she had a material enemy; her doubts vanished, and she said coolly:

'Keep your distance. I can hardly miss at this range.'

El Lobo said something quickly in Spanish. Almost before he had finished speaking, Alison heard soft footfalls behind her. She whirled about — too late! A dark face grinned at her and a strong arm went round her waist, pinning her arms at her sides. The Mexican took her gun away and tossed it over the cliff-edge, then released her.

El Lobo said: 'I like your spirit, Miss Knox, but I'm afraid I can't allow you to remain armed. I have only one life, and value it.' He tugged at his spade beard thoughtfully. 'I observe that Palmer is not with you — and I don't suppose you'll tell me where he is. As you see, I have your brother with me — but I would feel happier to know that Palmer was no longer free in the mountains.'

The Mexican who had appeared from behind Eagle Rock burst into a chatter of Spanish. El Lobo listened, his eyes moving from the bandit to Alison and back to the bandit. He smiled a little as he listened, then turned to the girl.

'Your brother tells me the next clue is here, at Eagle Rock. Have you found it?'

His voice was eager, his eyes searching her face. Alison shook her head.

'I looked for it, but couldn't find it.'

There seemed to be no point in concealing the fact she had failed to locate Seth Knox's clue. She waited, wondering what The Wolf would do.

El Lobo looked round at his men, a dozen strong, crowding the plateau under the shadow of Eagle Rock. He seemed to be deliberating.

'We shall go on to our hide-out,' he said at last. 'If the girl is lying, we shall persuade her to tell the truth — with her brother's life as forfeit. Velasquez, you will stay here and search. It should not take long to make sure the clue is no longer hidden here.'

Keith and Alison were mounted, guarded by dark-skinned bandits. El Lobo rode in the lead. They passed two horses, one the Mexican's who had been hidden at Eagle Rock; the other a big-boned bay horse. Alison gave a cry of recognition. It was Gil's horse.

El Lobo seemed amused. He said: 'You can forget your friend Palmer. He was careless enough to let my spy cut the rope he was climbing. He lies at the bottom of the canyon — dead!'

Alison went white. Her lips trembled and she felt faint. Gil — dead! She slumped in the saddle.

7

Gil Palmer did not have time to draw his guns. Velasquez's hurtling body crashed into him and sent him sprawling on the hard rock ground. The Mexican's knee dug into his stomach and one hand gripped his throat. The other was raised, carrying the knife, glittering in the sunlight.

Gil was weak from the arduous climb and in no condition for a hand-to-hand fight; but he had no option with Velasquez on top of him, intent to kill him. Gil could see clearly the livid scar starting at his jaw-bone and ending at his half-ear.

The knife plunged down . . . Gil's hands shot up, gripped Velasquez's wrist, turning it. The Mexican's momentum helped Gil — as Velasquez's knife whistled down, he rolled sideways, breaking the grip about his throat, turning the steel blade so that it clattered on the rock to one side.

Gil brought up his knee, rammed it into the Mexican's groin. Velasquez groaned and staggered back, giving Gil the chance to rise. He could have shot Velasquez in that moment, but he had no way of telling if other bandits were close, so he decided to finish the fight silently. He grappled with the Mexican, forcing him back to the edge of the cliff — his foot slipped and Velasquez took advantage of it. He was slim and panther-like and comparatively fresh; his swarthy hands jabbed into Gil's middle, knocking him back. Gil sprawled helpless, saw Velasquez poise for throwing his knife. The arm went back, swept forward, and the steel blade gleamed in mid-air, swishing, speeding for Gil's head. Gil flung himself wildly sideways; the haft of the knife caught his temple in passing, half stunning him.

Snarling, Velasquez went for his guns. Gil could have beaten him, even then, but a shot would have warned El Lobo, who could hardly be far away. Gil bent double and shot forward, head-first into Velasquez's stomach, his hands grabbing the Mexican's wrists, preventing him from shooting. Gil forced the guns from his hands, kicked them over the cliff. Then they were rolling on the ground, fighting for life in a bitter, tense silence.

Velasquez broke free, aimed a kick at Gil's head. Gil caught his ankle, twisted, bringing the Mexican to the ground. Gil leapt on top of him, slamming punches to the dark face, but Velasquez was tough. He took his punishment without a sound, writhing back, twisting and turning to escape Gil's hammering fists.

Velasquez swore in Spanish, blood dribbling from his mouth, a wild light in his eyes. Strong as he was, he realised he had met his match in Gil Palmer; now, his efforts were directed at escape. He scrambled away, with Gil chasing him over the rocky plateau.

The Mexican lurched in fight; his leg hurt from the fall and he could not run fast. Gil caught up with him, slammed him against the towering crag of Eagle Rock, battering him with his fists. Velasquez began to whimper, his nerve breaking. Gil fastened his hands about the dark throat, squeezing relentlessly, choking the air out of Velasquez's lungs.

He forced Velasquez to the ground, kneeling on him, tightening his hands about his throat. The Mexican saw the strained light in Gil's eyes; there was no mercy in Gil Palmer at that moment. He was an animal, lusting to kill, sweating with a tense expectancy. He no longer saw Velasquez's tortured face — he saw Alison, alone and menaced, and his grip closed savagely —

Velasquez made one last, desperate effort. He broke away, lunged wildly backwards, forgetting how near he was to the edge of the mountain — his feet slipped on the brink and he lost his balance, falling into space. His arms shot out in a frenzy of desperation; his voice whined:

'Save me — '

Gil leaned against the rock wall, panting for breath. The Mexican seemed to fall slowly; his feet appeared glued to the edge; his body moved out from the mountainside and his groping fingers missed the edge by inches. His feet fell free and he plunged downward — end over end, revolving.

His screams wailed horribly from the depths fading away as he plummeted down. The wind keened about him, drowning his scream, blotting out his death-cry. The silence grew — and lasted. Hundreds of feet below, Velasquez sprawled on the canyon bottom, broken like a toy doll — a strange, crumpled thing that a child might have thrown there. The days of El Lobo's lieutenant were ended.

By Eagle Rock, Gil Palmer sagged to the ground, exhausted. The tension went out of him, and he relaxed; gradually, his strength returned. He mounted Velasquez's horse and set off along the mountain track.

*   *   *

A slight breeze eddied about the mountains, bringing cooling relief to the bleached mesquite growing in rocky clefts. The path wound up and down, between soaring peaks, bordering a precipitous drop. In the distance the summits of other mountains along the range glittered and shone like faceted jewels.

Alison Knox passed all this with unseeing eyes. She was dimly aware of the stiff, proud figure of El Lobo, riding ahead; of Keith, at her side; of the chattering Spanish-Mexicans behind. Time and place meant nothing to her. She rode in a nightmare, not caring what happened to her; Gil was dead — and nothing had meaning any more.

The cavalcade moved on into the mountains. Far below, to the south, the Rio Grande wound like a giant snake;

to the east, the rolling plains of the cattle country sprawled, a dust cloud rising as a herd travelled overland; at the foot of the Sierra, the desert stretched out parched fingers, reaching clear to Paradise, a tiny dot in the vast panorama spreading out from the mountains.

El Lobo glanced back at Alison, smiling. His eyes gleamed as they rested on her youth and beauty; she wasn't at her best now, but he'd soon put a sparkle in her cheeks. The Wolf had big ideas where Alison was concerned — the self-styled king of the mountains needed a queen.

In the high altitudes the air was thin and hot, hazing into a mist. The riders passed between two towering crags, a guard posted on each. At their challenge, El Lobo answered in Spanish, and the cavalcade rode through the narrow gap. Beyond, the walls grew together to form the entrance to a cavern; this was El Lobo's lair.

They dismounted inside the cavern,

looped the reins of the horses to a hitching rack along one wall, in the shade. Farther into the cave, along a tunnel where another guard was posted, the passage opened into a vast hollow. Clefts in the walls and roof permitted sunlight to shine through, revealing the wooden shacks grouped about a crystal-clear stream tumbling down a fall of rocks. It was cooler here, out of the direct rays of the sun, an asylum made by some natural cataclysm of the past.

'My headquarters,' El Lobo said. 'A natural fortress, perfect for my needs. Here I am safe, because no man can reach me. From here my raiders strike at the surrounding country, loot and plunder, to return where no man can follow.'

Alison heard his speech, but the words did not penetrate to her brain. She showed no interest in her surroundings. The bandits took Keith and Alison to a shack, left them behind locked doors. The Wolf said:

'I shall give you audience later, after I

have rested and eaten — after Velasquez returns with the news from Eagle Rock. Till then, adios.'

There was a table and two chairs, a curtain across the window, an oil-lamp. Apart from these things, the hut was bare. Alison stood in the centre of the room, not seeing any of it. Keith guided her to a chair, made her sit down; he was worried about his sister and his face showed it.

'Snap out of it, sis,' he urged. 'We've got to get out of here somehow. They'll kill us, you know — kill us.'

She gave no sign that she heard him. A guard brought food and locked the door behind him.

'Eat something, Alison,' Keith pleaded. He pushed a plate towards her, sat down and ate himself. She pecked at the food automatically, not tasting it.

Keith said: 'I've something to tell you, sis.' He paused, watching her nervously. 'It's about Palmer — Gil, I mean. I didn't realise you cared so much about him, or I wouldn't have done it.' His words came out in a rush, as if he were afraid she might stop his confession. 'He left a message for you, saying he had gone after The Wolf, that he'd be back again. I destroyed it, thinking you would turn back east. I only wanted to go home, Alison; I didn't mean any harm. You'll forgive me, won't you?'

Suddenly, Alison seemed to understand what he had said. Gil hadn't deserted her — he had died trying to help her. She felt better, brightened a little. It would never bring him back, but at least she knew he hadn't deserted her.

'Of course I forgive you, Keith,' she said. 'It wasn't your fault.'

'I'm sorry about Gil.'

There was a silence, broken by the sound of the door opening. El Lobo entered, hatless.

'Velasquez has not yet returned,' he said. 'That may indicate you were telling the truth — that the clue to the treasure is still hidden there. I hope so.

I should hate to use persuasive methods on one so fair — yet, if it were necessary, I should not hesitate.'

Keith said: 'You swine! Keep your hands off my sister!'

He was scared of The Wolf, but, with Gil dead, there was no one else to protect her. He advanced on El Lobo, hands clenched, young face white and strained. El Lobo laughed mockingly.

'No harm will come to your sister — if I get the gold. She is lovely — and a white woman, the first I have known for many years. I, too, had a sister — once.'

He brooded, stroking his beard, looking into the past.

'I was in the army, an officer in the cavalry. I had money, high position, power. Then my sister was tricked by a scoundrel — he married her, got hold of her money, and deserted her, leaving her with a sick child, penniless, and in hostile country. The child died — and my sister committed suicide!'

El Lobo paused, his eyes gleaming coldly.

'That man — I shot him in a duel. But he was a sheriff — and I became a man with a price on my head, an outlaw with every man's hand turned against me. I travelled south, to the border country.

'I was an army man, trained to command men, to make war — and I was at war with the society that had murdered my sister and proclaimed me an outlaw. I formed my gang, trained Velasquez to see that my orders were carried out, and started my campaign. For years I have been terrorising the border, stealing cattle and selling them in Mexico, robbing banks, holding up the mail coaches. Yes, I have had my revenge — and grown rich in the process. Now, I am king of the mountains; here, my word is law!'

Keith snapped: 'You're mad!'

Alison, who had been fascinated by El Lobo's revelations, said gently: 'But you've murdered innocent men and women. Do you think your sister would have wanted that? Don't you — '

'Quiet!' The Wolf snarled. 'Not one of them is innocent — they all have the blood of my sister on their hands! And they'll pay for it — and go on paying as long as I can ride a horse and shoot a gun!'

His face was livid with emotion. Alison shrank back, afraid; this thing had preyed on his mind till he was no longer able to think straight — he used the death of his sister to ease his conscience, to give him an excuse for killing and plundering. He was, as Keith had said, mad —

El Lobo made an effort to regain his composure. He stiffened, fighting his burning passion for revenge. He forced a short laugh, looking at Alison with a new interest.

'You understand, don't you? I'm a lonely man, Alison — but I shan't be alone any more. I'm rich; I can give you everything you want. I am going to do you the honour to make you my wife, Alison!'

The girl's face paled. She said calmly: 'I presume I have no choice in the matter?'

'Choice?' El Lobo laughed. 'I am king of the mountain, and it is my prerogative to chose whom I will — and I chose you. You will never leave these mountains now. I know you fancied yourself in love with Palmer, but you'll get over that. You'll come to love me, Alison!'

Keith was horrified at the position his weakness had placed his sister in.

'You can't force her into a marriage she doesn't want!' he burst out. 'I won't let you — I'll kill you!'

He threw himself wildly at El Lobo. The Wolf moved back, drawing his gun.

Alison shouted: 'No! Keith, he'll — '

El Lobo reversed the gun in his hand; struck the youngster across the head with the butt. Keith moaned and dropped to the floor stunned. The Wolf holstered his Colt and took a step towards the girl.

Alison backed against the wall, afraid of what she saw in his eyes. Her despondency left her; her sadness at Gil's death was submerged by other, stronger feelings. She was a woman defending herself against a man who intended to force his attentions on her.

'If you touch me,' she said, 'I'll kill myself!'

El Lobo laughed, gripping her wrists and dragging her towards him.

'I thought you'd show a little more life, my beauty! You'll forget Palmer soon enough — '

She fought against him, but his strength was greater than hers. He crushed her slim form to his chest, forcing her head back. His face loomed above her; his lips pressed down, fastened on her mouth in a long, intense kiss.

El Lobo drew back his head, gulping down air. He flung Alison back against the wall, laughing. He wiped his lips with a silk handkerchief and said: 'I like your spirit. I like a girl with plenty of spirit — but I'll tame you!'

There came a knock at the door — an unexpected interruption.

* * *

Velasquez's horse was a sure-footed gelding, used to the mountain trails, and Gil had no difficulty riding it, even though the ornate Mexican saddle was higher than his own. He got used to riding without stirrups, too, with his feet dangling at the gelding's flanks. He rode with one hand loose on the reins, the other touching the butt of a Colt .45, Seth Knox's map in the forefront of his mind.

It was easy to follow the route left by the Aztecs, for the mountains had changed little with passing centuries, and there were few trails branching off. Gil thought it ironic that probably El Lobo had ridden this same trail many times without realising the wealth that lay hidden close by. But it was no use

trying to pick up The Wolf's scent —
the bare rock would show no marks
even if a regiment had ridden there.

In that wilderness of mountain he
could search for weeks without finding
the man he sought — and with Alison's
life at stake, time was vitally important.
So Gil put thoughts of Alison from his
head and concentrated on finding the
hidden treasure — with that as bait, El
Lobo would come a-running into his
trap.

The narrow path wound between
rocky overhangs, dipping into hollows,
rising again on the bluffs, winding in
and out of the mountain range. The
view was magnificent; the air hazed
with the heat of the sun.

He recognised landmarks from the
map he had found near Seth Knox's
skeleton. Along the trail, where it swung
inward from the sheer drop to the
canyon floor, he saw two towering
crags, like sentinels, one each side of
the path. He tingled with excitement;
this was the opening to the cave where

the Aztecs had buried their sacred treasures.

He passed between the crags, thinking of the plan he had formed to trap El Lobo, his mind confused by the picture of a pretty young girl with red hair and tawny eyes, when something seemed wrong. Beyond the opening there were hoof-marks in the dust. Fresh hoof-marks.

Gil stiffened, a chill creeping along his spine. He halted his horse, his eyes searching the gloom of the cave entrance, hand tight round the butt of his holstered Colt. Danger threatened; he could sense it. There came a whirring sound faint in the air above his head. He looked up, tried to duck sideways — too late. The rawhide lariat came down over his shoulders, tightened, imprisoning his arms and dragging him out of the saddle.

High on the towering crag, the Mexican guard grinned down at him, hauling on the rawhide. He shouted in Spanish, and other swarthy-faced bandits appeared. Gil's Colts were taken from him, his hands bound at his back. It was useless struggling with knives and gun-muzzles digging into him. He groaned inwardly. What chance had he now of saving Alison? He was still shocked by his capture. There could be no mistake. He had followed the directions of the Aztec map, located the treasure cave — and found El Lobo's hide-out.

Spanish tongues questioned him, gesturing at Velasquez's horse. Gil shrugged, unspeaking, his mind busy with the new problem. One Mexican, a newcomer, took one look at Gil and howled. His hands shook, his eyes bulged.

'*Madre de Dios!* It ees Señor Palmer returned to life. I myself cut the rope that sent him falling to the canyon bottom. It is a ghost come to haunt me!'

The guard who had lassoed Gil laughed scornfully and prodded his captive with a knife.

'See, the blood runs red. This is no ghost, you fool — you imagined you killed this señor.'

But the other Mexican was not convinced. He backed away, crossing himself and muttering under his breath. The contagion caught and, for a moment, Gil thought they might take to their heels and run. But the guard was a materialist. He said:

'We will take this ghost to Señor Wolf. He will know how to deal with a ghost — El Lobo fears nothing.'

Gil was pushed along a dark tunnel opening into a rock-covered hollow. Sunlight, filtering between cracks in the high walls, showed the huts built around a waterfall. Gil was staggered. There was no doubt in his mind now — this was the treasure cave. The waterfall, marked on the map, proved it. El Lobo had discovered this hiding-place, as the Aztec Indians had done, centuries before — but The Wolf had no idea he was camped on the site of a fabulous lost treasure. And Gil wasn't going to tell him . . .

His guard knocked at the door of one of the shacks, opened it after an exchange of Spanish, and Gil was pushed inside. For the second time, he came face to face with El Lobo. Gil's eyes passed beyond The Wolf. He glimpsed Keith, unconscious on the floor, and Alison, white-faced and trembling, huddled against the far wall. His breath came out in a sigh of relief when he saw that she was not hurt.

Both Alison and El Lobo were taken aback at the entrance of the man they had thought dead. Alison ran across the room, crying:

'Gil! Gil — they told me you were dead. I'm so glad — '

She nestled to him, her arms round his neck, kissing him.

'A touching reunion,' El Lobo jeered. His expression changed. 'The fool who said he had killed you will be punished for this slip, Palmer. Now tell me, how is it you rode here on Velasquez's horse?

I'm sure he didn't make you a present of it.'

'You'll find Velasquez at the bottom of the canyon with his neck broken — and there's no mistake about that. Yore Mexicans are lousy fighters, El Lobo.'

The Wolf's face darkened with anger. Veins stood out on his forehead.

'You'll pay for that with your life, Palmer. It took me a long time to train Velasquez; now I've got to start again to train a second-in-command. These Mexicans do not take easily to army discipline — you've put me to a lot of trouble, and you'll regret it.'

He leaned forward, thrusting his bearded chin at Gil.

'Now tell me — the treasure. Did you find the clue at Eagle Rock?'

'There is no clue at Eagle Rock,' Gil stated calmly. 'You're wasting yore time looking for it.'

'Don't play with me, Palmer. Remember, I've got the girl — and you wouldn't like anything unpleasant to happen to her, would you?'

'Leave Alison out of this. You touch her and I'll fill you so full o' lead that even the vultures won't feed on yuh! This is between you and me. Give me back my guns and we'll shoot it out, man to man.'

His challenge caught El Lobo by surprise. The Wolf laughed.

'You fool! Do you imagine I'll give you the chance to escape? You'll die — after I've got the secret of the treasure. And Alison will be my wife.'

Beads of sweat stood out on Gil's brow. He wrestled with his bonds, but they had been securely tied; he could not free himself.

'I'll kill yuh, El Lobo — I'll kill yuh for sure. Alison's too good for a renegade, a turncoat who leads murdering greasers against his own people.'

El Lobo struck Gil across the face.

'You — you talk to me like that! Me, the king of the mountains — '

'King — nothing!' Gil spat back. 'Untie my hands and try that again.

You're no better than a greaser yoreself.'

El Lobo strived to control himself. He succeeded, after an effort.

'I won't hit you again, Palmer. That was a slip.'

'You bet it was,' Gil taunted him. 'And not the first one, either. Yore days are numbered — the Texas Rangers are on to yuh. Maybe you'll kill me — and remember, I'm not dead yet — but there'll be others on your trail. One of them will get you.'

The Wolf stood motionless, surprised. Then he laughed softly.

'So you're a Ranger? That's why you're riding the border — falling in with the girl was just a blind. Well, Texas will be a Ranger short from now on. If you caught me, I'd swing — what's sauce for the goose — '

He swung round, snapped orders in Spanish, then turned to Alison.

'I've given word to prepare a gallows. How would you like to see your lover swinging in the breeze?' He chuckled. 'I

241

think you'd do what I want. With Palmer to play with — and your brother — I think I'll get the gold — and you!'

Gil swore bitterly. 'Tell him,' he said, 'to go to hell!'

Alison looked at Gil, her face pale, then at the floor. Her lips moved, but her words were too low for anyone to hear. She was praying.

'The gold,' El Lobo demanded. 'Where is it?'

'I've told you,' the girl said defiantly. 'I never found the clue at Eagle Rock.'

The Wolf smiled and wheeled about to face Gil.

'Ah, yes. She never found the clue — because you got there first, Palmer. That's it, of course.' He stared at Gil thoughtfully. 'I could force you to speak by torturing the girl — but I don't want to spoil her looks. As you know, I've certain plans for Miss Knox.' He looked at Keith, sprawled unconscious on the floor. 'But her brother now. Suppose one of my men applied a little — persuasion. Alison will break down —

and you'll talk to save her feelings.' He rubbed his hands, pleased with his scheme.

Gil said: 'I know where the treasure is, El Lobo — and I'm the only one who knows, because I destroyed the map, committing the hiding-place to memory. So you can leave both Alison and Keith out of this. It's between you and me now — and you'll never force me to talk.'

The Wolf said: 'No?'

'No. But I'll make a deal with you. Release Alison and her brother, give them horses and provisions and set them free — and I'll tell you where the Aztec gold is buried.'

Gil waited, tense, wondering if El Lobo's greed would come to the fore, if it was greater than his lust for the girl.

Alison said: 'I won't leave without you, Gil.'

El Lobo looked from Gil to Alison, and laughed. 'It would be a pity to separate you,' he said softly. 'Such devotion is touching. No, your bargain does not interest me, Palmer — I shall find another way of loosening your tongue.'

Gil's heart sank. He almost groaned aloud, and had to struggle to keep his face calm, so that Alison would not see how hopeless he felt. The treasure he cared nothing for — El Lobo could have that. Gil's only concern was to save Alison, to get her out of The Wolf's power — and it looked as if he had failed.

El Lobo gave orders in Spanish, and Gil and Alison were tied, back to back, in the two chairs. Keith was bound and left on the floor. The Mexicans left the shack. El Lobo paused in the doorway, and said:

'I'll leave you to think it over. I hope you'll be sensible, Palmer, and save a lot of unpleasantness — I mean to have the gold.' He grinned. 'If you hear hammering, it will be my men, erecting a gallows for you!'

He went out, locking the door behind him. There was silence. Outside, men worked with wood and nails, hammering away happily; to lynch a lawman was the Mexican bandits' idea of fun.

Gil drawled: 'Don't give up hope, Alison. We're not dead yet.'

He heard her voice, from behind him.

'I'm sorry I got you into this, Gil. And for what I thought about you when I imagined you'd deserted me. I'm not afraid to die — and I shall kill myself if El Lobo forces me to marry him.'

'Stop thinking like that,' Gil said sharply. 'While I'm alive, El Lobo won't touch you. And I aim to stay alive a long time yet.'

Alison said calmly: 'I want you to know Gil, before the end — I love you.'

'And I love you, Alison. I guess I always have, since I set eyes on yuh in Smoky Joe's saloon.'

He struggled with his bonds, refusing to let himself give up hope. He cursed in a low monotone all the time, then remembered Alison. He said:

'We'll be married as soon as we get out of here.'

She made no sound, but he could feel her body heaving, and guessed she was crying. Keith moaned faintly, and moved on the floor. His eyes opened, stared up at them. After a time, he grinned and said:

'So they didn't kill you after all, Gil!'

'Save yore energy for getting those ropes off,' Gil commanded. 'We ain't got much time, afore El Lobo comes back for the showdown.'

Keith moved on the floor, wriggling, but his bonds were secure. The three captives were helpless.

Keith said: 'This is my fault, Gil, and I want you to know I'm sorry. I've misjudged you all the while. I think you're one of the finest men I've ever met.'

There was another silence, except for the incessant hammering outside the shack. Someone was singing in Spanish.

Keith said: 'I suppose it's not much use my saying it — but I'd do anything to put myself square with you, Gil.'

Alison said: 'It seems strange how curious I am, at a time like this, but — did you find the clue at Eagle Rock, Gil?'

'Better than that — I found the map.' He told her how he'd found her grandfather's skeleton and followed the map's route.

Alison's reply was startled: 'Then the treasure is here? In this cave?'

Gil laughed grimly. 'Yeah — and El Lobo will never know!'

The hammering stopped. There were footsteps; the door opened and El Lobo and two Mexicans came in. Gil felt the hairs on his neck rise.

El Lobo said: 'The gallows are ready, Palmer. Say your last prayers!'

8

One of the Mexicans used a knife on Gil's cords, releasing him from the chair. He stood up, flexing his muscles, facing El Lobo, coolly calculating his chances. His hands were still bound and bandits gathered in the doorway, laughing and making jokes. If he could kill El Lobo, the greasers would run like frightened rabbits. Already he had undermined their morale by killing Velasquez — it was only The Wolf's strict discipline, his commanding presence, that made them a deadly fighting unit.

He was marched outside, to the gallows erected in the centre of the hollow. He stood against the wooden post while they placed the rope about his neck; he dare not make a break yet — there were too many guns covering him. Alison and Keith, their hands tied similarly, were brought out to watch. Alison's face was pale, but she kept her chin well up.

Gil stood with his back to the centre post of the gallows, his hands behind him. He leaned back a little — and hope began again. The Mexicans were no carpenters — and someone had driven a long nail clear through the framework; its sharp point pricked Gil's wrists. He worked the rawhide thongs binding him against the sharp nail; now, if only something would detract their attention for a few minutes —

El Lobo left Alison's side and walked across to the gallows, facing Gil. His white shirt, riding breeches and boots were as immaculate as ever; his eyes gleamed and he stroked his spade beard with an air of satisfaction. Gil eyed him calmly, stopping work on his bonds.

'Murdoch is dead, his outfit smashed,' The Wolf said. 'You alone stand between me and the treasure, Palmer — but not for long.' He paused, gloating over his victim; El Lobo saw Gil as the lawman who had driven his sister to suicide. 'This hanging is not going to be the usual affair. There will be no sudden drop, no quick death by broken neck for you. When I give the word, you will be slowly hauled off the ground, an inch at a time. The rope will tighten about your neck, choking you, slowly and painfully. You will have plenty of time to reconsider telling me the hiding place of the gold.' Gil didn't answer him. El Lobo went on:

'You can save yourself a lot of pain by talking now. Remember, Miss Knox will be watching your death struggles — you will wish to save her feelings as much as possible, won't you?'

Gil's face was calm; gently, he worked the rawhide binding his wrists behind him against the nail. Already he could feel the strands giving. Time was what he wanted —

Keith said: 'There's no need for all this. I know where the gold is — I'll tell you, El Lobo, if you promise to release me!'

The Wolf turned — and Gil attacked his bonds furiously. All eyes were on Keith Knox now. Alison snapped:

'Shut up, Keith — don't tell him anything. Talking won't save you now — can't you see that?'

El Lobo said: 'How do you know? If this is a trick, you'll regret it. You were with me when Palmer reached Eagle Rock.'

'Palmer told us after you left us alone — spare my life and I'll talk.'

Keith's face was alight with eagerness: it seemed he was willing to sacrifice Gil — and his sister — to save his own skin. The Wolf's lip curled in disgust.

'Well, talk!'

Keith held out his bound hands.

'Cut me free and I'll lead you to the gold. You can have it — all I want is to get out of this horrible country, to go back east.'

'Talk first — I'll set you free afterwards.'

Alison stared at her brother with

bitterness in her heart.

'You fool, Keith — don't trust him!'

Gil worked at his bonds; the nail dug into his flesh and blood ran down his hands — but he was getting free. Not much longer — if only Keith could keep El Lobo's attention distracted.

'Are you afraid I'll attack you?' Keith sneered. 'Don't tell me The Wolf is afraid of one unarmed man!'

El Lobo quivered with anger; his right hand dropped to the Colt .44 hanging at his waist. He stared icily at the youngster who had dared speak to him in that manner — this weakling who had proved himself a coward many times over, and was now willing to sacrifice his own sister.

'Turn him loose,' he ordered abruptly.

A Mexican cut the rope about Keith's wrists; guns swung to cover the youngster as he rubbed his hands to renew the circulation in them.

El Lobo demanded: 'Now where is this treasure?'

There was a tense silence while Keith

looked round him. Alison stared back at him, pity in her eyes. Gil worked silently at the nail behind him, slicing through the rawhide thongs about his wrists.

Keith turned to Alison, and said in a clear voice: 'I've got to do this, Alison. It's my last chance — '

His voice faded away. He tensed — then he leapt forward, grabbing at the nearest Mexican's gun. Shots blasted out, ripping into him. He tore the gun from the surprised bandit's hand and swung the muzzle to point at El Lobo. The hollow echoed to a barrage of revolver fire; shells smashed into Keith's body as he tried to aim at The Wolf. He was sagging, coughing blood, his face dead white; it was only sheer will-power that kept him on his feet.

El Lobo realised his danger. By rights the kid should be dead — but desperation lent him courage. He was determined to kill The Wolf first to save his sister. El Lobo's right hand moved. He drew and fired in one swift movement; his shell struck Keith's gun-hand, sent the gun spinning away from him. The Mexicans continued to pour lead into the youngster's body till it lay motionless and bleeding on the ground.

Keith had made his bid — and failed. But in failing, he had proved himself a man — and given Gil the time he needed. Alison was staring in horror, her face white as a sheet, tears streaming down her cheeks. Her choked sobbing was piteous to hear. El Lobo holstered his .44 after pushing a fresh shell into the empty chamber; he looked at the girl, and looked quickly away.

Gil tore the last strip of rawhide from his wrists, ripped the noose from his neck, and went into action. Keith had sacrificed his life in an attempt to protect Alison — and Gil was determined his sacrifice should not be in vain. Grim-faced, he hurled himself at the guard holding the gallows rope; the Mexican was taken completely by surprise, and Gil got his guns and started spraying lead into the bandits.

Hell broke loose under the rock-encased cavern. Startled by Keith's desperate attempt to shoot down their leader, the Mexicans were not prepared to see Gil break loose from the gallows. Before they collected their senses, Gil had dropped three of them in their tracks.

The gang broke into panic, running wild, their Spanish voices screaming, guns blazing lead in all directions. Only El Lobo kept his head; he spun round to face Gil, checked himself as he saw the Texas Ranger's gun point at him. His arms dropped loose at his sides, and he called bitterly: 'So you'd shoot me down in cold blood?'

Gil held his fire, sweating. This was the moment he had dreaded. They were alone in the cave; all The Wolf's men had fled. Alison crouched over her brother's dead body, crying softly, cradling his bloody head in her arms. Gil and El Lobo faced each other —

and Gil knew he could never shoot down The Wolf without giving him a chance.

'Put your hands up — and keep them up!' he ordered. El Lobo obeyed.

Gil smiled coldly, snatched up a dead man's gunbelt, and fastened it about his waist. He holstered his guns, and said: 'You can lower yore hands, El Lobo. When you're ready, we'll shoot it out. I'm not figgering on taking yuh alive!'

They stood, twenty feet apart, tense, each waiting for the other's move. El Lobo held himself stiffly, his face calm, his manner assured; even though his position had changed with lightning speed, this proud man showed no sign of weakness. The Wolf was sure of the speed of his gun-hand, waiting to test it against the Ranger's.

Gil crouched, his arms bent, hands hovering motionless above the butts of his twin Colts. He knew again that nervous tension he always felt when about to kill. He too, had confidence in the speed of his draw.

Alison looked up, saw the two men facing each other. Her voice rang out: 'Kill him, Gil — kill him!'

Her voice was an echo inside Gil's head. Slowly the cavern walls seemed to recede. The light, filtering down from the roof, pin-pointed a rigid, proud figure, a white shirt, and bearded face. He saw only his target.

El Lobo saw the way Gil shook, watched the sweat run down his face — and thought Gil was afraid. He laughed softly — and his eyes revealed he was ready to draw. Gil waited till movement came — The Wolf's right hand travelled fast and his .44 came out spitting lead.

Gil's hands seemed to turn outwards — and he suddenly had a gun in each. The cave echoed to thunderous sound as Gil triggered out .45 shells, straight for his target. The Wolf fired once — and a rush of wind whipped past Gil's head.

El Lobo staggered, surprise in his face. His gun-arm dropped. Gil kept on firing, pumped lead into the white shirt, watching a red stain spread across it. Abruptly The Wolf crashed to the ground.

Gil swayed, breathing heavily. Death had passed close by to seize El Lobo in its tentacles. He holstered his guns and wiped the sweat from his face and hands.

His gaze shifted from the dead body of The Wolf to Alison, crouched beside her brother. He picked up a knife and cut the ropes about her hands, looked down at Keith. The youngster's face was strangely calm and proud in death. Gil bowed his head.

'I reckon,' he said slowly, 'that yore brother had real guts. You and yore grandfather can be proud of him. He died like a man!'

Alison's eyes shone through her tears. She slipped into Gil's arms, clung there. His lips touched hers, then gently he pushed her away.

'Wait in the hut while I make a grave. Then I'll take you out of this.'

Gil found a place where earth spread a brown layer over the rocks and scooped a shallow grave. He buried Keith, and Alison said a short prayer over the grave. She was suddenly calm and composed now that it was over.

Gil said: 'Murdoch won't bother us, according to The Wolf. And the Mexicans will still be running for the border; with their leader dead, they won't have any heart left in them. I reckon we can head east without trouble — and maybe stop in at the Rileys' place?'

She nodded. 'And the treasure, Gil — it's here? After all, it's what I came for, and Keith and grandfather gave their lives to find it. There's no point in leaving it now.'

He turned, staring across the cavern to where the waterfall tumbled down from rocky heights.

'I don't suppose you'll mind a ducking? The directions on the map show another cave — beyond the fall.'

Alison joined him as he waded into

the pool at the bottom of the fall. The water was shallow and clear, and spray drenched them. Gil walked into the spray, feeling the rock wall behind it. His groping hands found an opening, and he passed through. It was pitch black beyond.

'Wait here,' he told the girl. 'I'll get a lamp.'

He returned to the shack and found an oil-lamp, lit it, and draped oilskin round the glass to protect it from the water. He went back through the fall to Alison. In the yellow light from the lamp he saw a small cave, low-roofed, and extending hardly more than ten feet into the cliff face. The floor, and niches in the wall, gleamed gold and silver — they had found the Aztec treasure, lost for three centuries.

There were plates and chalices of pure gold; bowls and vases of silver; sacred idols, wrought in precious metal with the most exquisite workmanship; piles of golden coins; statuettes, orna- ments, feminine trinkets; swords and knives and jewelled hilts; even small things like spoons or cups were of gold, decorated and embellished with great artistic skill.

Alison's eyes shone as she handled individual items.

'This isn't just a treasure hoard, Gil. The value of these things can't be judged in gold or silver — they are art treasures, wonderful examples of the art of a dying race. To museums and art galleries, to collectors, these treasures are priceless.'

Gil smiled faintly.

'I'm willing to take their value in gold. Me, I'm not a great lover of art. Though,' he added, admiring a silver statue, a representation of one of the Aztec gods, 'they look mighty fine! Maybe we'll keep one or two for the home.'

They carried the treasures out to the larger cavern and Gil packed them carefully on horses and mules the bandits had left behind. They set off down the mountain, riding north-east with their string of treasure-laden mules, detouring to avoid the desert crossing. Days later, they arrived back at the Twisted T.

Tom Riley and his wife welcomed them back.

'Where's Keith, your brother?' Riley asked the girl.

Alison's face clouded. It was Gil who replied.

'Keith was buried up in the mountains. We had a set-to with The Wolf — and he proved himself a man.'

Riley was excited. 'El Lobo? What happened to that coyote?'

Gil touched his gun-butts.

'The Wolf ain't a-going to bother anyone again. He's rustled his last steer — and the border is safe for honest folk.'

'My, that's a relief,' Martha sighed. 'I guess you two are dying of hunger. You rest up a while and I'll fry some ham and eggs!'

She bustled away, taking Alison with her. Riley wanted to know about the fight, and Gil told him in terse sentences. His job was over now; he could report back at headquarters and tell his chief that El Lobo was a back number. There were other outlaws, of course, but none so dangerous. Gil had something else on his mind; he was going to turn in his badge and hang up his guns. Younger men could ride the trail, carrying law and justice to the West. Gil thought of a quiet ranch where he and Alison could live together as man and wife, enjoying the peaceful years ahead. Martha called from the house and the two men went in to join the women.

Over the meal Martha turned to Alison and asked:

'What are you going to do now? Go back east, I suppose. When I was a young girl I — '

Tom Riley kicked his wife under the table.

'It's a fine moonlit night,' he observed casually, 'and if I was younger I'd be out there enjoying it.'

Gil grinned, and took Alison's arm. She went without a struggle out through the porch to the veranda. Silver moonlight flooded the mesa and cottonwoods swayed gently in the breeze; the scent of sage and tumbleweed drifted across the prairie and cattle lowed in the distance. It was suddenly hushed; a stillness settled over everything, and Gil took Alison in his arms.

Her eyes were a beautiful tawny, her lips red and full and parted expectantly. Gil kissed her and held her close.

It was instinctive — something he had wanted to do for quite some time. She made no move to stop him. The light in her eyes told him all he wanted to know — told him she loved him.

But Gil slowly released her. He moved back a pace as if he had presumed too far. She gazed at him, puzzled, apprehensive.

'Guess I shouldn't!' he said thickly.

'Reckon I'm the one to decide that,' she retorted.

He shook his head. For the first time

she saw him undecided and irresolute, and it mystified her completely.

'What's wrong, Gil?' she asked softly.

He hesitated and wetted his parched lips.

'Guess we can't have everything we want in this world,' he said awkwardly.

'Don't talk in riddles!' she said sharply. 'Just say what's on your mind.'

He just stood there, wrestling with words that teemed in his brain. It wasn't easy for a man of action to speak all his thoughts.

And as she stood there, watching him, the truth dawned in upon Alison.

'If it's the treasure — ' she began.

He nodded gloomily.

'You're rich,' he said. 'Me — ' He didn't complete the sentence, merely shrugging his shoulders ruefully.

Alison's eyes blazed.

'What does that matter?' she flashed back. 'I'll give everything away — everything.'

'You mustn't,' he argued. 'After all you've been through to get it.'

'You endured as much as I did. But for you the treasure would never have been found. But if it's a matter of choice I'd sooner not have the treasure!'

There was no mistaking her meaning, yet his doubts still persisted — but he was wavering.

'Alison darling, you know I want to marry you, but — now — the treasure — '

She tossed back her red hair.

'You've as much right to that as I have. We'll share it — or give it away! And if you think you can get out of marrying me, you seriously underestimate the Knoxes!'

She laughed softly.

'You're hooked, Gil — and it's no use wriggling. I made up my mind to marry you quite a while back, so — kiss me again!'

The moon passed behind a cloud and darkness fell over the prairie. When the silver radiance shone again, it revealed a man and a woman silhouetted against

266

the western hills; they stood close together unspeaking, their faces showing delight at the new treasure they had found.

A treasure that had nothing to do with border gold.

THE END

We do hope that you have enjoyed reading this large print book.

Did you know that all of our titles are available for purchase?

We publish a wide range of high quality large print books including:
Romances, Mysteries, Classics
General Fiction
Non Fiction and Westerns

Special interest titles available in large print are:
The Little Oxford Dictionary
Music Book, Song Book
Hymn Book, Service Book

Also available from us courtesy of Oxford University Press:
Young Readers' Dictionary
(large print edition)
Young Readers' Thesaurus
(large print edition)

For further information or a free brochure, please contact us at:
Ulverscroft Large Print Books Ltd.,
The Green, Bradgate Road, Anstey,
Leicester, LE7 7FU, England.
Tel: (00 44) 0116 236 4325
Fax: (00 44) 0116 234 0205

DUEL OF THE OUTLAWS

John Russell Fearn

The inhabitants of Twin Pines, Arizona lead uneventful, happy lives — until the sudden arrival of Black Yankee and his gang. They shoot the sheriff, take over the place, and Twin Pines spirals downwards into an outlaw town, with lawlessness and sudden death the norm. When Thorn Tanworth, son of the sheriff, returns from his travels, to everyone's astonishment he establishes a mutually beneficial partnership with Black Yankee. But then the two men begin fighting each other for control of the town . . .

KID FURY

Michael D. George

The remote settlement of War Smoke lies quiet — until the calm is shattered by a gunshot. Marshal Matt Fallen and his deputy Elmer spring into action to investigate. Then another shot rings out, and cowboy Billy Jackson's horse gallops into town, dragging its owner's corpse in the dust: one boot still caught in its stirrup, and one hand gripping a smoking gun. Meanwhile, the paths of hired killer Waco Walt Dando and gunfighter Kid Fury are set to converge on War Smoke . . .

FIVE SHOTS LEFT

Ben Bridges

When you have only five shots left, you have to make each one count. Like the outlaw whose quest for revenge didn't go quite according to plan. Or the cowboy who ended up using a most unusual weapon to defeat his enemy. Then there was the storekeeper who had to face his worst fear. A down-at-heel sheepherder who was obliged to set past hatreds aside when renegade Comanches went on the warpath. And an elderly couple who struggled to keep the secret that threatened to tear them apart . . .

VENGEANCE TRAIL

Steve Hayes

A vengeance trail brings Waco McAllum to Santa Rosa, hunting his brother's killers: a grudge which can only be settled by blood. He finds valuable allies in Drifter, Latigo Rawlins, and Gabriel Moonlight — three men who are no strangers to trouble. But along the way, he finds himself on another trail: a crooked one that leads straight to a gang of violent cattle-rustlers. In the final showdown, will Waco get his revenge — or a whole lot more besides?

A ROPE FOR IRON EYES

Rory Black

Notorious bounty hunter Iron Eyes corners the deadly Brand brothers in the house with the red lamp above its door. As the outlaws enjoy themselves, Iron Eyes bursts in with guns blazing. But Matt Brand and his siblings are harder to kill than most wanted men: they fight like tigers, and Iron Eyes is lynched before they ride off. Yet even a rope cannot stop Iron Eyes. And he is determined to resume his deadly hunt, regardless of whoever dares stand in his way.

THE BANDAGED RIDERS

Gordon Landsborough

In the shambles of the stricken, defeated South, lawless men like Reuben Slatt and his ragged followers roam free. Slatt has an idea: adopt the flag of the victors to forcibly take over a town, bleed the place dry, and shoot as traitors any Southerner who dares raise a hand against them. But there is one man who will not stand by and see people exploited and humbled. And yet he knows nothing about himself — not even for which side he had fought during the war . . .